THE DAY OF RECKONING
BY

MICHAEL A. ANGELICOLA

The Day of Reckoning is a throwback to
old school action horror movies and
video games, such as Night of the
Living Dead and Resident Evil.
As you read the story you will notice
several nods and easter eggs to many of
my favorite horror movies. I wanted to
write a story that pays tribute to all
the director sand authors before me who
were able to create a genre that
everyone could enjoy. So I have taken
my love for that genre and added my own
spin on things. I sincerely hope you
have as much fun reading this as I had
writing it. It was a blast!

Thank you.
Mark A. Angelicola Jr.
Octavia Orciari
and Shawn Costello
With out you guys pushing and
supporting me through out all this none
of it would be possible. Thank you all
so much.

CHAPTER 1:

SPACE:

An object is floating around EARTH. It looks like a satellite.

CRAVEN ISLAND/MORNING:

A small island off of CALIFORNIA. There were a couple towns on the island,the most popular being DINOSAUR VALLEY. It was a small peaceful community with farms,no crime and everyone knew each other. There was a small building with multiple apartments. Inside was a man who was tossing, turning and covered in sweat. "BEEP BEEP" His alarm clock waking him up! He shot up and sat there shaking and whipping the sweat from his face. He then slowly got out up bed and headed to his bathroom. As he walked, he stumbled passed empty beer bottles on his floor. He turned on his shower and and looked into his mirror. He was his mid thirties with black hair and a goatee with a light five o' clock shadow. He was powerfully built and rougish good looks. He had multiple scars covering his body. Inside his apartment were beer bottles on his table, counter tops and floor. He had military awards and medals on his walls and few on his shelf. On the night stand next to his bed, as a picture with him and a woman. They both looked very happy together.

<u>**DINOSAUR VALLEY/MORNING:**</u>

There was a fishing dock where the ferry ports to bring people on and off the island. A boat went by, on the side of it read "The ARGENTO". On it was a man with a cigar in his mouth. He was wearing a baseball cap which read "Fish 'n' Chips".

<u>**DINOSAUR VALLEY/MORNING:**</u>

In the middle of town there were people coming out of the local grocery store, DV-Mart. Outside was a young man pushing carts. Down the street was "BUB'S PUP". Across the street was "LUCIO'S APIZZA". There was a police car was making its rounds. The patrol car pulled into the police department. Out stepped the same man from the apartment.

<u>**DINOSAUR VALLEY POLICE PRECINT:MORNING**</u>

He entered the department. There was a woman sitting at a desk. She was in her early thirties, with curly light brown hair and an unbelievable smile.

ASH:
"Morning Curtis."

LAURIE
"Morning Redfield."

They both smiled at each other, revealing they had some kind of past together.

ASH:
"Let me guess, nothing interesting again
today?"

LAURIE:
"Let me check."

She looked at her computer screen. She
then smiled looking back at ASH.

LAURIE:
"Well it looks like the same thing we
had yesterday."

ASH:
(Sarcastically)
"Nothing?"

LAURIE:
(Sarcastically Back)
"Yeah, and even more nothing."

ASH:
(Sighing)
"Well I'm going to my desk."

LAURIE:
"Enjoy you're day."

ASH walked over to his desk and sat down.
He placed his feet up on his desk and
his hat over his eyes. He then crossed
his arms. LAURIE began to laugh. ASH
then flicked her off.

ELSEWHERE OUTSIDE/MID-DAY:

A family getting ready to move.

There was a van full of luggage with a
man was yelling. He was also in his mid
thirties. He had brown hair and a light
five o clock shadow.

ELSEWHERE INSIDE HOUSE/MID-DAY:

A woman is standing at the bottom of a
set of stairs. She had long brown hair,
was in her early thirties. She was
calling up to someone.

BUFFY:
"Sarah, come on Hun. We need to hurry up
were going to miss the ferry."

SARAH:
"Ok, Mom I just have to get my suit
case."

The man came into the house soaked with
sweat. He took a rag out of his left
back pocket. He began wiped his face
with it.

ERIC:
"This is bullshit Buffy, I told her to
get her shit ready and by the door last
night."

SARAH was at the top of the stairs
dragging her suitcase. She was about ten
or eleven. She had her mother's brown
hair. She looked down at her mother and
BUFFY looked up at her.

SARAH:
"I'm ready!"

She began to drag the suitcase down the
stairs. It slipped out of her hands. The
suitcase came tumbling down the stairs.
It crashed into the ERIC'S right knee.

ERIC:
"Son of a Bitch!"

SARAH:
"I'm sorry daddy, it slipped."

SARAH ran down the stairs and hid behind
her mother. The man began to lunge at
the little girl. BUFFY stepped in the
way.

BUFFY:
"Eric, the suit case was too heavy for
her, it's not like she meant for it to
hit you."

SARAH placed her hands around her mother.
BUFFY put her hand on the girls head.

ERIC:
"Well, maybe if she did some housework
instead of being on the phone all the
time she wouldn't be such a bitch!"

BUFFY:
"Eric, watch your mouth. Why do you have
to be so mean? She's a
child let her have her friends."

ERIC:
"When I was her age I was helping my
father mowing the yard and chop logs."

He stood there rubbing his leg. BUFFY couldn't help but crack a smile.

ERIC:
"I didn't have time for friends and look how I turned out."

BUFFY:
(Mumbling Under Her Breath)
"Yeah, look at that."

BUFFY went to walk away. ERIC grabbed her by the wrist yanking her out of SARAH'S grasp.

ERIC:
(Aggravated)
"What is that suppose to mean?"

BUFFY:
(Scared)
"Nothing, Eric, it didn't mean anything."

SARAH:
"Mom, we're going to be late."

BUFFY:
"Alright honey, we're leaving"

She said this she yanked her arm free of ERIC'S grasp. Then held her wrist. ERIC grabbed SARAH'S suit case and stomped out the front door. He bumped into SARAH on his way out causing her to fall to the floor. She looked up at her mother with tears in her eyes...BUFFY walked up to SARAH. She then looked at ERIC by the van. She was hoping that this new place would be a new beginning for them.

SARAH:
(Holding Back Tears)
"Why does daddy have to be such an ass?"

BUFFY kneeling beside her. Then extended
her hand out for her to grab.

BUFFY:
"Watch your mouth. Daddy's just having a
bad day, that's all."

SARAH reached for her mothers hand.
BUFFY picked her up and brushed her pant
leg off.

SARAH:
"He sure does have a lot of bad days."

The tears in SARAH'S eyes were gone.
BUFFY eyes started to swell. She turned
around and looked into the house, it was
completely empty. The only presence that
anyone lived there, was the Spackle on
the walls that covered the holes that
were made. BUFFY then turned around. She
grabbed the door handle as she did this
she answered SARAH.

BUFFY:
"Yeah, I know baby."

ERIC:
(Outside)
"Let's get going now!"

She shut the door behind her.

<u>**CRAVEN ISLAND/ DV MART:AFTERNOON**</u>

There were two people inside of what
looked to be a storage room. The guy was
buttoning up his pants. The girl was
putting her panty's on. They looked as
if they just got done having sex. The
guy was about eighteen or nineteen, dark
skinned and had long dread locks. The
girl was around his age, she had golden
long blonde hair. Her face and body were
to die for. The man looked at his watch.

JAMES:
"Shit Stephanie, Mr. Campbell's gonna
kill me. My break ended fifteen minutes
ago."

She rolled her eyes and gave a sigh.

STEPHANIE:
"Relax James, it's not the end of the
world. Besides wasn't it worth it?"

She walked up and gabbed his crotch.
They both smiled.

JAMES:
"Yeah, it was."

They quickly kissed.

JAMES:
"I gotta go."

He walked out the door. She continued to
get dressed.

DINOSAUR VALLEY PORT:DUSK

The sun was setting and a handful of
boats were entering a port. The ARGENTO
pulled up and the man with the cigar
jumped off. Took off his hat and
scratched his head. His crew tied down
the boat. The man was blonde and
scraggly looking. He looked like he
could use a nice hot shower an about a
years rest. He walked up to a door that
read MR. SNYDER on it and waked in.

DINOSAUR VALLEY PORT MAIN OFFICE/DUSK:

A man was sitting at a desk. He was late
thirties early forties,
with light brown hair and a rough five
o'clock shadow.

MR. SNYDER:
"Ahh, Mikhail my favorite Russian. Here
you go."

He tossed him an envelope. MIKHAIL
opened it up. He looked shocked, then
threw his hands up in disappointment.

MIKHAIL:
(Russian Accent)
"What's this?"

MR. SNYDER:
"What's what?"

MIKHAIL:
"This, where's my money?"

MR. SNYDER:
"It's there, you're lucky I gave you
that."

MIKHAIL:
"But all that fish."

He pointed out the door where a large
line started to form.

MR. SNYDER:
"I pay you buy the pound, and you didn't
have that much."

He lit up a cigar. Then blew the smoke
at MIKHAIL.

MR. SNYDER:
"There are taxes, what you owe me and
you're using my boat. It all adds up."

MIKHAIL:
"This is bullshit!"

MR. SNYDER:
(Slamming His Hand On His Desk)
"No, do you wanna know what's bullshit?
I give you a boat, to get me fish. No
fish, no money, capche!"

MIKHAIL:
"Yeah, yeah whatever."

MR. SNYDER:
"Good, I'm glad we understand each other.
Now send Chaz and A.J. in here."

MIKHAIL walked out slamming the door.

<u>**DINSOAUR VALLEY PORT/DUSK:**</u>

As MIKHAIL down the dock, he bumped into
someone.

MIKHAIL:
"Hey, Chaz. Snyder wants to see you and
A.J."

CHAZ:
"What's up?"

MIKHAIL
"Everything but the pay."

CHAZ:
"Are you serious?"

MIKHAIL:
"Yeah. Anyway, where's captain queasy?"

CHAZ:
"Still throwing up."

MIKHAIL:
"I don't know why you take him with you?"

CHAZ:
"He makes me laugh."
(He Chuckles)

MIKHAIL:
(Light Chuckle)
"So what are you and Megan doing this
weekend?"

CHAZ:
"Don't know probably sit around and drink

a twelve pack."

MIKHAIL rolled his eyes as they both
laughed.

MIKHAIL:
"Well I'm outta here. I'll see ya
Monday."

CHAZ:
"Alright, take it easy man."

They went they're separate ways.

L.A. DOCK:NIGHT

The MERCER family just missed the last
ferry. He was yelling at the person at
the counter.

ERIC:
"You gotta be fucking kidding me! Can't
it turn around?"

MAN:
"Sorry, you guys are gonna have to wait
until tomorrow. When it
makes it's round back."

ERIC:
"What fucking time?"

Nervous, the man shuffled around some
paper.

MAN:
"Ahh... around nine. If you want there's
a hotel across the street."

ERIC walked away. He got into his car
slamming the door behind him. BUFFY knew
something was wrong by the way she
stormed towards the car.

ERIC:
"Well we're fucked."

BUFFY:
"What do you mean?

ERIC:
"We missed it."

BUFFY:
"When's it coming back."

ERIC:
"Nine tomorrow."

BUFFY:
"So what are we gonna do?"

ERIC:
"We're gonna have to sleep in the
fucking hotel across the street."

He then turned around and looked at
BUFFY.

ERIC:
"If I miss this interview Sarah, I swear
on my life you're gonna be sorry."

SARAH'S eyes opened wide with fear.
BUFFY couldn't believe what she heard.
ERIC started the car. He pulled out of
the driveway.

And headed across the street to the
hotel. Meanwhile in the sky there
was an object that looked like a
shooting star. Only it wasn't a shooting
star, it was the satellite. As it hit
the atmosphere there was large orange
flash in the sky and a ripple through t
he clouds. And the satellite itself was
coming down right above CRAVEN ISLAND.

RESSURECTION CEMETERY/NIGHT:

There was a man sitting by a grave. He
was a lightly dark skinned man, with a
long goatee and an Afro that was way out
of control. The tomb he sat next to read
"JORDY VERILL". Nabgeta had a small
bottle of alcohol and a small bag.

NABGETA:
"You know it's just not the same without
you Jordy. Yea you were a fuck up, but
still you didn't deserve what you got.
But seeing how it's your birthday I got
you a nice birthday pie!"

He pulled a small pie out of the bag. He
took a piece and placed it on the
gravestone.

NABGETA:
"Here was it down buddy."

He poured the alcohol on the grave. The
NABGETA went to bite his slice of pie.
Suddenly there was a bright light above
his head. He looked up and saw the
satellite falling right above his head.

NABGETA:
(Sighing)
"You know Jordy, you were always bad
luck."

CRASH!
The satellite landed right on top of
him, killing him instantly. There was a
loud crash and after the dust cleared
the was a strange eerie orange glow
coming off of it.

<u>**CHAPTER 2:**</u>

<u>**DINOSAUR VALLEY/BUB'S PUB:NIGHT**</u>

ASH was sitting there with a shot glass
in front of him.

ASH:
"Here's to my two best friends, Jack and
shit. Cause that's all I
got left."

He took the shot. Then the bar tender
came up to him. He was very handsome and
just one look from him would drive any
woman wild. He had black hair, with a
thick beard. The name tag on his shirt
read SETH.

SETH:
"Alright Ash, you're on duty. I can't
give you anymore."

ASH:
"Is this it?

SETH:
"Ash, you know you can't hold your
alcohol."

ASH:
"No, is this what I was kicked out of
the service for? A dead job in a no name
town. For god sakes we're not even on
the map."

SETH:
"Come on it's not that bad."

ASH:
"I've been the deputy here for a year
now, and you know the only excitement I
get?"

With a heavy sigh, SETH decided to amuse
his brother.

SETH:
"What?"

ASH:
"Getting Old Man Lombardi's cat out of a
tree once a week. That's it."

He slammed his glass on the table.

ASH:
"Christ, I'd rather take my chances in
Sona."

SETH:
"It was fun when we were kids."

ASH:
"Well I want some adventure. I'm tired of
getting drunk in this place."

SETH gave ASH a insulted glance. ASH
quickly took notice.

ASH:
"No offense."

Elsewhere in the pub. MIKHAIL was
sitting with CHAZ, A.J. and MEGAN.

MIKHAIL:
"I think you've had enough Meg."

MEGAN:
(Slurring)
"I'll tell you when I've had enough. I
mean who does he think he is? Telling me
I can't do my job. I know teacher. I do
teacher. I AM TEACHER!"

A.J.:
"Easy now, Meg."

He tries to take her bottle away. But
she pulls back.

CHAZ:
"I wouldn't do that if I were you,
remember last time A.J.?"

A.J.:
"Oh yeah, never underestimate a kick to
the groin."

MIKHAIL:
"How many is that now Meg?"

MEGAN:
(Completely Gone)
"I DRANK A TWELVE PACK!"

RESSURECTION CEMETARY:NIGHT

The place the satellite fell into
earlier,a group of people entered it.
There were five friends. Three guys and
two women.

COREY:
"What do you wanna do Joe mess up some
gravestones?"

JOE:
"I just wanna look around the graveyard.
I never seen one before."

COREY:
"You never been to a funeral?"

JOE:
"I never knew anybody that died."

They began to walk around. Little did
they know what was happening in the
cemetery around them. In another part of
the cemetery hands began popping out of
the ground. Whatever chemical was in the
satellite caused the dead to come back
to life. They started crawling out of
their graves. Mausoleums doors were
pushed opened. Corpses barely holding
themselves together came walking out. A
crypt in the middle of the cemetery lid
was being pushed off. A corpse's head
popped out, it was rotted and flesh was
barley hanging on. The corpses began
walking around.

Back with the group of friends. They were
sitting around a fire and drinking beer.

RAY:
"Why did Stephanie say she couldn't come
again?"

She pulled out a joint and began to roll
it.

KELLEY:
"Not couldn't, wouldn't. She's seeing
someone now."

She lit up the joint and began to smoke
it. She then passed it on to her friend
NINA.

RAY:
"Who?"

NINA:
"That guy who works at DV-Mart. James, I
think."

COREY:
"Sorry, you waited too long dude."

KELLEY:
"If it makes you feel better she seemed
like a snobby bitch."

RAY felt began to feel like shit. NINA
then offered him the joint
and he refused.

RAY:
"Well it doesn't."

KELLEY just shrugged her shoulders. She
knew he wasn't going to be easy to get
along with tonight.

KELLEY:
"I tried"

RAY got up and began to walk off.

KELLEY:
"Where are you going?"

RAY:
"To get more beer, it's gonna be along night."

He walked off. COREY and NINA began to walk off too.

JOE:
"What about you two?"

NINA:
"We're gonna go look around.

JOE:
"And?"

COREY:
"Use your imagination, I'm gonna get stiff with the stiffs."

They both walked off into the darkness.

JOE:
"It's about damn time."

He moved closer to Kelley, putting his arms around her.

KELLEY:
"What about Ray?"

JOE:
"What about him?"

KELLEY:
"Hey, he's feeling really lousy, and he needs to be around people."

JOE:
"Well what do you want, I have my needs
too ya know."

She sat on his lap. He then pulled up
her shirt and stuck his face in between
her breast. Back at the car RAY was in
the trunk. He pulled out a six pack and
shut the trunk. When he turned around he
was confronted by a person, you couldn't
see it's face in the dark.

RAY:
"Whoa, buddy you kinda gave me scare."

The person didn't respond. RAY noticed
blood falling to the ground.

RAY:
"Hey, you ok?"

The person came into the light. He was
grotesque looking. Pieces of rotting
flesh looked as if it was pealing off of
it's face. His eyes had dark circles
around them with a blank stare. With
maggots was pouring out of it's mouth.

RAY:
"What the?"

The persons mouth went wide showing dirt
stained teeth. He lunged at him pushing
him up against the trunk. Then took a
huge chunk out of RAY'S throat. RAY
pushed the person back. He then began to
run but he stumbled and fell face first.
He turned around on to his back.

When he looked up he saw more of them
surrounding him. They all lunged at him.
In another part of the cemetery COREY a
nd NINA were making out. He had her
press up against a tree. She was pulling
at his shirt. They were both wrapped up
in the moment. Then suddenly COREY was
grabbed by the back of the head. He was
pulled into the darkness. There were
sound of biting and clawing mixed with
his screams. Before NINA had a chance to
react a decayed hand grabbed her head.
It rammed it back in the tree branch
causing the branch to go through her
eye. With JOE and KELLEY. She lifted her
head off of JOE'S lap.

KELLEY:
"What was that?"

JOE:
"What? I didn't hear anything."

JOE pushed her head back down on to his
lap. KELLEY sat up and wiped her face.

KELLEY:
"No, hold on I heard something. Could
you check on it and get more wood the
fires going out."

JOE:
"I got all your wood right here."

Grabbing his crotch and smiling. She
pushed him back.

KELLEY:
"I'm serious, and besides Ray will be
back any minute."

JOE:
"Fine!"

Realizing he'd never win this argument,
he got up and buttoned up his pants. He
walked off in to the woods. KELLEY
shouted out to RAY.

KELLEY:
"Ray, can you bring back my hoodie?"

There was no answer.

KELLEY:
"Ray?"

She got up and walked toward the car.

KELLEY:
"Ray, you there? This isn't funny."

Still no answer. In the woods JOE was
talking to himself. Unaware of the group
of zombies circling around him.

JOE:
"Fucking women man, I'll never
understand them, when your hot they're
cold."

KELLEY walked up to the car but couldn't
find RAY. She went around the front and
heard a chewing noise. Then she couldn't
believe what she saw.

There were about four people on top of
RAY and they were eating him. His chest
was ripped open along with his rib cage.
They were fighting over his intestines.
One ZOMBIE was wearing a green jacket
who has a bald, white, diseased-looking
head. It was crouched over RAY,
apparently eating the poor soul. The
ZOMBIE took a soft bite, then a loud
one, which causes a puddle of blood to
ooze out over the ground. The ZOMBIE
then slowly turns its head to look at
KELLEY with bloody lips. A small piece
of intestines fell out of it's mouth and
hit the ground with an uneasy sploosh.
KELLEY let out a loud screamed. JOE
heard it from with in the woods. He
turned around and saw a group of people
around him.

JOE:
"Hey!"

The people tackled him. He tried to
fight back but there were too many. They
began biting him and ripping him apart.

JOE:
"Run Kelly! Run!"

Then a ZOMBIE put its hand into JOE'S
mouth. It ripped out his tongue. Then
they pulled his jaw off.

KELLEY, hearing his cries got into the
car and locked the doors.
She went to start the car, but then
realized JOE had had the keys.

KELLEY:
"Fuck!"

The ZOMBIES began to attack the car.
Violently shaking it.

KELLEY:
"Go away! Help me!"

They broke the windows. Her screams
echoed through the night.

CHAPTER 3:

DINOSAUR VALLEY/BUB'S PUB:NIGHT

ASH was still sitting down, SETH looked
at him while cleaning a glass.

SETH:
"You really miss her huh?"

ASH:
"What are you talking about?"

ASH was trying to pretend he had no idea
who SETH was talking about. But SETH saw
right through his bullshit.

SETH:
"You know, Diana? Christ, how long has
it been? 5, 6 years?"

ASH:
"8 years, 2 months and 3 days."

SETH:
"Just remember Ash, she thought you were
dead. Hell we all did. I was devastated
and so as she. But she moved on and
moved to LA to become some big shot
journalist."

ASH just sat there an was moping and
brooding, just trying to ignore SETH.

SETH:
"Ash, you were missing for two years.
What else did you expect her to do?
She's just as strong willed as you are.
Not to mention stubborn too."

ASH
"She could have reached out to me anytime
since I've been back. Ball was in her
court."

SETH:
"Okay you have me there. But haven't you
thought, maybe she got married?"

ASH was shocked at this remark. He never
even thought of that
before.

ASH:
"Thanks buddy, keep throwing salt on the
wound there. When you're done with that
perhaps you'd like to poke me in the eye
with an umbrella?"

ASH held up a tiny umbrella from a
margarita glass. He then tossed
it at SETH.

SETH:
"Hell I'm even surprised you can even
lift that glass. You've been carrying
that torch for so long."

ASH:
"That reminds me, there's something I've
been meaning to tell you."

SETH:
"What's that?"

ASH signaled for SETH to come closer.

ASH:
"Fuck you, asshole."

SETH rolled his eyes and just walked
away. While ASH was just sitting there
an old man sat next to him. He was in a
preachers robe with four other people.
He had a light white beard and very
short white hair. He also had on a very
thick pair of glassed. He looked
at ASH.

FATHER ROMERO:
"What troubles you my son?"

ASH:
"You don't want any of my problems,
padre. Trust me."

FATHER ROMERO:
"I'm am never one to judge son. Just
like the lord. He is always willing to
listen, just as I am."

ASH sighed heavily knowing there was no
way out of this conversation.

ASH:
"Ok, padre you win. My first problem is
that I'm all outta beer and my brother
Seth refuses to give me anymore because
I'm on duty."

FATHER ROMERO:
"Well it seems to me that your brother
has the right idea. How can you do any
good for the people when you can barely
stand?"

ASH:
"You'd be surprised at what I can do."

FATHER ROMERO:
"Well when the end of days comes, for
your sake I hope so."

ASH:
"The end of days.....? I think you've
been reading that good book, mumbo jumbo
to much."

FATHER ROMERO:
"It's not wise to mock ones religion
officer. Especially one who
will lead us in our darkest hour."

ASH:
"No offense padre, but from where I'm
standing, your savior aint leading but
two things right now. Jack and shit. And
jack left town."

FATHER ROMERO:
"I'm sorry you feel that way. So tell me
when the end of days comes, what will
you be doing?"

ASH:
"I hope to high hell I go with a cold
beer in one hand, a greasy pizza in the
other, and god willing a beautiful broad
on my lap. All while watching reruns of
the big comfy couch."

FATHER ROMERO looked at ASH and smiled.
ASH then backed away from
the counter and put his hat on.

ASH:
"Well I'd better get back before Curtis
throws a fit. I'll see you tomorrow."

A very large man approached ASH. He as
bigger than ASH, a towering over him and
extremely built. He was bald and a bushy
beard.

SAVINI:
"Excuse me officer, but I believe you owe
this man an apology."

ASH looked at him confused.

ASH:
"For what exactly?"

SAVINI:
"He's a preacher? He deserves your
respect."

ASH:
"And he has it, but I'm sorry but me and
the man upstairs don't exactly see eye
to eye. Not that it's any of your
concern buddy. So if you don't mind,
I'll be on my way."

ASH turned around to leave, then
suddenly SAVINI grabbed ASH by the
shoulder.

ASH:
"Take your hand off me."

SAVINI:
"Not until you apologize."

ASH quickly turned around and pushed the
hand right off. SETH notice and ran in
between them.

SETH:
"What's the problem here guys?"

ASH:
"I'm just trying to take off, but King
Kong here won't let me."

SAVINI pushed SETH aside and got right
into ASH's face.

SAVINI:
"What did you say to me?"

ASH:
"I believe it was something to do with
the amount of hair on your neanderthal
body, Kong."

SETH jumped back in between the two of
them.

SETH:
"Enough!"

SETH looked at ASH.

SETH:
"You go, now! I'll see you later."

He looked to SAVINI.

SETH:
"You sit down and have a drink. On the
house."

ASH looked a little shocked at this.

ASH:
"He gets a free drink?"

SETH looked into ASH's eyes.

SETH:
"Please, just go."

ASH saw the seriousness in his brothers
eyes and agreed to go.

ASH:
"Fine."

ASH went to leave but then looked over
at FATHER ROMERO.

ASH:
"Good luck with your whole end of days
thing, padre. Let me know how things
turn out."

ASH walked out of the pub. SAVINI looked
over at SETH.

SAVINI:
"You should have just let me kick his
ass."

SETH looked at SAVINI.

SETH:
"Trust me, I just saved yours."

SAVINI stood there puzzled by the
remark. ASH made his way outside where he
was greeted by and old man.

ASH:
"Oh great, what now Mr. Lombardi? If Mr.
Whiskers is in a tree he can wait until
morning."

MR. LOMBARDI:
"No, I saw something in the sky."

ASH:
(Not Interested)
"Really?"

MR. LOMBARDI:
"Yes, it was on fire. I think it landed
over in Prospect."

ASH:
(Sarcastically)
"I think you need to lay off the booze."

MR. LOMBARDI:
(Shaking His Cane)
"I know what I saw you little punk."

He began to hit ASH with his cane.

ASH:
"Ok, ok. I'd hate to have to haul you in
for assaulting an officer."

MR. LOMBARDI:
"Then we'll you check it out?"

ASH:
"I guess, I'll call Prospect and see if
they heard of any great balls of fire
landing ok?"

ASH got into his car. MR. LOMBARDI
looked at him.

MR. LOMBARDI:
"Thank you."

ASH:
"No problem."

MR. LOMBARDI:
"Also one more thing.

ASH:
"What's that Mr. Lombardi?"

MR. LOMBARDI:
"Mr. Whiskers is in my tree."

ASH:
(He Sighed)
"Of course he is. I'll get him down."

MR. LOMBARDI turned around and began to
walk away. ASH shook his head and
smiled.

ASH:
"Damned ol' booze hound. Seriously
what's with all the crazy shit tonight?"

He drove off.

DINOSAUR VALLEY PRECINT:NIGHT

ASH entered and saw LAURIE.

ASH:
"It's nice to see you busting your ass."

LAURIE:
(Sarcastically)
"Well, someone's got to do something
around here. Where were you?"

ASH:
"Out and about."

She rolled her eyes.

LAURIE:
"I'm sure you were."

ASH:
"I'm calling it a night. You should too."

LAURIE:
"Yeah."

ASH was heading out the door when the
phone rang. LAURIE answered it.

LAURIE:
"Hello? Uh-huh. Are you sure? Ok."

She yelled to ASH.

LAURIE:
"Hold it!"

ASH popped his head back in.

LAURIE:
"We'll send someone as soon as
possible."

ASH looked at her confused.

ASH:
"What?"

She put her hand over the phone.

LAURIE:
"There were some screams by the cemetery
in Prospect, you gotta check it out."

ASH:
"Get Sheriff Hooper on it."

LAURIE:
"Can't he's at the Landona farm, cow
tipping."

ASH:
"Cow tipping? People seriously still do
that?"

LAURIE:
"Yeah. I guess so."

ASH:
"Do I have too? I Just want to get back
to my loft and get drunk."

LAURIE:
"Do this quick and you can."

ASH:
(Tired)
"Fine, I'll check it out."

LAURIE:
(Talking Into The Phone)
"Someone will be there shortly. You're
welcome. Goodnight."

She hung up.

ASH:
"You really want me to go out there?"

LAURIE:
"It's you're job."

ASH:
"My job is to find criminals, not break
up teenage orgy's."

LAURIE:
"Oh, you know you like it."

ASH:
"You wish."

LAURIE:
"Stop pretending I wasn't the best you
ever had."

ASH was headed toward the door.

ASH:
"Stop pretending I even remember."

LAURIE:
"Stop pretending!"

He walked out the door giving her a
friendly flick off.

LAURIE:
"Would that be one o'clock?"

The door shut and she sat at her desk.
ASH left.

LAURIE:
"Asshole."

He jumped into his car and drove off.

RESSURECTION CEMETARY:NIGHT

Fifteen minutes later he was at the cemetery. He saw a car sitting there and got out. Pulling out his flashlight, he began to look around. He saw the windshield shattered and blood all over ground.

ASH:
"What the fuck happened out here?"

He slowly pulled out his gun and made his way around the car. Then he tripped. He took his flashlight, pointing it to where he tripped. He saw what was left of RAY'S body. He jumped up.

ASH:
"Fuck me!"

Then there were noises all around him. He pointed his gun and stood there waiting. It was too dark to see anything. Suddenly he was attacked. Something jumped on his back and he quickly threw it off. Then he scrambled around on the ground for his flashlight. When he found it he stood up pointing it in front of him. It was KELLEY, her face was torn apart. Part of her lower lip was gone with scratch marks all over her face. Her shirt was ripped and chunks of flesh were missing. ASH pointed his gun at her.

ASH:
"Come any closer and I'll fire."

She moved toward him.

ASH:
"I mean it!"

She kept coming. ASH sighed then shot
her in the left leg. BLAM! She looked
down at her leg then back at ASH. He
looked confused that she was still
standing. He then shot her in the right
leg. BLAM! Again she kept coming.

ASH:
"Fuck it."

He then shot her in the chest
repeatedly. BLAM! BLAM! BLAM! She flew
back. ASH then stood there trying to
figure out what was going on. Soon there
were the sounds of footsteps. He turned
around and saw more of the ZOMBIES.

ASH:
"Shit."

He made his way toward his police car.
He walked by the body when it grabbed
him by the foot. He dropped his
flashlight. Luckily the headlights from
the teens car were bright enough for him
too see. He looked down and shot her in
the head. The other ZOMBIES lunged
towards him and he began to fight them
off. During the scuffle the head lights
off the car started to dim. There was
too many of them and they tackled him to
the ground. Soon the headlights died. It
was pitch black then all that was heard
was the moaning of the ZOMBIES.

ASH screamed. Then after a few seconds
his gun went
off. BLAM!

<u>**CHAPTER 4:**</u>

<u>**NEXT DAY/CARPENTER CEMETERY:EARLY MORNING**</u>

There were two guys digging a grave.
Behind them there were three tombstones.
The names read, MICHAEL, JASON, and
FREDDY.

GUY #1:
"You know the great thing about this job
is?"

GUY #2:
"What?"

GUY #1:
"You get to meet new people every day."

They both laughed.

GUY #2:
"You know who this guy was?"

GUY #1:
"No, but wanna find out?"

They both lifted the top off of the
coffin. The guy inside looked a lot like
VINCENT PRICE.

GUY #2:
"Did you know this guy?"

He then looked down and noticed a gold
watch.

GUY #1
"Oh, look at the watch!"

He went to take it off.

GUY #2:
"What are you doing?"

GUY #1:
"What?"

GUY #2:
"You can't do that?"

GUY #1:
"What? He's not gonna be needing it."

GUY# 2:
"I don't need the money that bad, I'm
outta here."

He began to walk off.

GUY #1:
"Come on who's gonna know? Him? Besides
check out this ring.

GUY #1 picked up the corpses hand.

GUY#1:
"Aint it a beauty!"

GUY #2 looked and then grabbed the ring.

GUY #1:
"Well let's close this thing before
someone sees us."

As they went to close it, the guy in the
coffin eyes opened. He shot up and
attacked GUY #1 biting him the ankle.
GUY #1 scrambled out of the hole.

GUY #2:
"What the hell?"

GUY #1:
"Help me, get him off of me!"

GUY #2 then grabbed GUY #1 by the arms.
He tired to pull him out of the hole.

GUY #1:
"Get him off of me! Ahh!!"

GUY #2 was still tying to pull his
friend out of the hole. Then something
grabbed him from behind. Scared, he
flipped around to see anther ZOMBIE. He
lost his grip on his friend. His friend
fell back into the hole. Where the guy
in the coffin began to biting him. The
ZOMBIE bit him in the face and ripped
his eye out. GUY #1 let out a painful
scream and GUY #2 ran for dear life.

<u>ELSEWHERE:EARLY AFTERNOON</u>

An empty road there was ERIC'S van.
ERIC, glanced at the clock on the radio.

ERIC:
"Fuck, We're going to be late."

BUFFY:
"We'll make it."

She looked at the gas meter.

BUFFY:
"We'd better get some gas."

ERIC:
"What else can go fucking wrong?"

They pulled into a nearby gas station.
ERIC and BUFFY got out.

BUFFY:
"Sarah, you wait right here."

BUFFY waited by the car and filled up
the tank. ERIC entered the gas station
called BIG DADDY'S GAS. Inside it was
completely trashed.

ERIC:
(Mumbling Under His Breath)
"Fucking hicks."

He looked around but couldn't find
anyone.

ERIC:
"Hello, anyone there?"

There was no answer.

ERIC:
"I need to buy some gas. Hello?"

Again. There was no answer.

ERIC:
"Listen, I'm in a hurry so I'm gonna
leave the money on the counter."

He walked up to the counter and heard a
chewing noise. He looked over the
counter and saw the GAS TENANT.

ERIC:
"Hey, what's the matter with you?"

The GAS TENANT slowly turned his head.
His mouth was covered in blood. The GAS
TENANT just got done eating the CASHIER.
The GAS TENANT name tag read BIG DADDY.
BIG DADDY looked at ERIC. ERIC ran out
the door. BUFFY saw him running towards
them.

BUFFY:
"What's wrong?"

ERIC:
"Get in the car Buffy, now!"

BUFFY:
"What is it Eric?"

ERIC:
"The gas tenant killed the cashier!"

BUFFY:
"What!"

ERIC:
"Let's get the fuck out of here!"

SARAH was looking out the back window.

She saw people coming from behind the
gas station. On the other side of the
road coming out of a corn field. BUFFY
got to the car when she was grabbed. She
turned around and saw a ZOMBIE. The
ZOMBIE grabbed her hand and put it into
her mouth. She began to freak out. She
ended up ripping the ZOMBIES jaw off in
the process. The ZOMBIE staggered back
and BUFFY jumped into the car. ERIC
started it up and they drove off.

DINOSAUR VALLEY WOODS:EARLY AFTERNOON

GUY #2 was running through the woods
like a bat outta hell. There were
ZOMBIES all over the place. He ran pass
them pushing aside. He then approached a
tree to catch his breath. Suddenly two
hands came around a tree and grabbed
him. He jumped back and pushed the
ZOMBIE.

GUY #2:
"Get away! Stay back!"

He struggled passed the ZOMBIE, who
slowly followed him. He then saw the
center of DINOSAUR VALLEY from the
woods. He gave a sigh of relief. Then he
slowly made his way to the road.

GUY #2:
"Come on, you're almost there."

Suddenly his leg was grabbed.

GUY #2:
"What?"

He looked down and saw a ZOMBIE holding
on to his leg.

GUY #2:
"No! Let go!"

He tried to shake of the ZOMBIE. Then
more came from around the tree. GUY #2
grabbed a branch from off the ground and
began to swing it around.

GUY #2:
"Get away, stay back!"

A ZOMBIE then grabbed GUY #2 by the
throat. Then he tore the flesh off. GUY
#2 began to choke on his blood. The
ZOMBIE'S dragged his body to the ground.
Then tore him to shreds.

DINOSAUR VALLEY/BUB'S PUB: NIGHTFALL

It was a usual night at the pub. People
just sitting around and bullshitting. At
the table in the corner was MIKHAIL was
sitting with his crew. Over at the bar
was SHERIFF HOOPER, He was a black
man in his late forties, early fifties.
Bald head, thick goatee and mid weight.
He was talking with SETH.

SHERIFF HOOPER:
"It's not like Ash to be like this. He
never misses a day's work."

SETH:
"Did you go to his loft?"

SHERIFF HOOPER:
"Twice, I've been calling him all day.
No answer. Curtis said he went out to
Prospect to check on some screaming
kids."

SETH:
"You know what I think happened then? I
think he brought one of them home and
decided to take the day off."

SHERIFF HOOPER:
"Well he'd either better be getting the
best pussy of his life or he'd better be
dead."

They both began to laugh. Then the pub
door opened, a person with his head
looking down slowly entered. No one was
paying any attention. They were to busy
in their own worlds. SETH looked at the
person, then at SHERIFF HOOPER.

SETH:
"What a weird customer."

SHERIFF HOOPER turned around and looked
at the person.

SHERIFF HOOPER:
"I don't think he's a regular."

SETH:
"Yea, possibly a drunk?"

SHERIFF HOOPER:
"I'll handle this, you just try and get a
hold of your brother."

SETH:
"Will do."

SETH went to use his phone. SHERIFF
HOOPER he then casually walked up to
person.

SHERIFF HOOPER:
"Can I help you?"

There was no response. The person just
stood there blankly.

SHERIFF HOOPER:
"Hey buddy, can I help you? Is something
wrong?"

The person lifted his head up and showed
a decade face.

SHERIFF HOOPER:
"Son of a bitch."

The ZOMBIE quickly lunged at SHERIFF
HOOPER and tackled him to the ground.
Everyone jumped up and began to freak
out. SETH looked over and saw what was
happening. He dropped his phone and ran
up to the SHERIFF. The ZOMBIE bit
SHERIFF HOOPER in the throat and tore
the flesh off. Blood squirted everywhere.
Then there was banging on the door as
more ZOMBIES were outside the Pub.
Everyone inside ran out the door in a
panic, But the ZOMBIES were pouring
inside and attacking everyone. SETH
managed to grab SHERIFF HOOPER'S gun.
Then a WAITRESS was knocked over, she
landed on the floor by some feet.

When she looked up she saw a ZOMBIE and
she screamed. MIKHAIL looked and quickly
thinking grabbed the fire axe and ran up
to the ZOMBIE. He swung the axe and hit
the ZOMBIE in the shoulder and kicked
the ZOMBIE back. Then he looked down at
the WAITRESS.

MIKHAIL:
"You ok?"

WAITRESS:
(Nodding)
"Uh-huh."

MIKHAIL:
"Come on, it's not safe here."

He grabbed her hand and ran up to SETH.

MIKHAIL:
"Is there a back door out of this
place?"

SETH:
"Follow me."

They followed him behind a door.

DINOSAUR VALLEY/OUTSIDE: NIGHTFALL

All hell is breaking loose. They were
everywhere, people were running and
screaming. A small van pulled up and
inside was the MERCER Family.

ERIC:
"What the fuck is going on?"

BUFFY:
"Maybe we should head back Eric?"

Then suddenly a ZOMBIE came crashing
onto their hood. BUFFY and SARAH
screamed. ERIC hit the gas and drove
like a mad man.

BUFFY:
"Eric slow down!"

ERIC:
"Shut up, Buffy!"

The ZOMBIE smashed the windshield. ERIC
began to drive blindly and argue with
BUFFY. He then drove right into a road
sign. The ZOMBIE flew off and was
impaled on a broken pipe. BUFFY slowly
picked up her head and then turned
around.

BUFFY:
"Sarah! Sarah!
Oh, my god are you ok!"

SARAH:
"Yes, I'm fine."

BUFFY:
"Are you sure?"

ERIC:
"We need to get the fuck outta here."

They all got out of the van and began to
run. The ZOMBIES were everywhere.

They pulled one lady out of her car, and
tore her apart. Another man was running
towards a church. Just as he made it to
the door the ZOMBIES grabbed a hold of
him. They pulled him down and ripped
into him. His guts were all over the
church side walk. Then a mother and her
kids were surrounded by a couple of
ZOMBIES. The mother tried to protect
them. She swung her grocery bags around,
but the ZOMBIES over powered her. They
were pulling people out of cars.
Smashing through store windows killing
who ever got in there way. Somewhere in
the chaos, ERIC, BUFFY, and SARAH were
running. ERIC looked over and saw some
ZOMBIES pulling someone in half. The
ZOMBIES digging in to his stomach.

DINOSAUR VALLEY/POLICE PRCEINT:

LAURIE was looking out the windows and
seeing all the carnage that was
happening outside. All the phones were
ringing and she couldn't figure out what
was going on. She then saw a little boy
standing outside the front doors. She
ran and opened them.

LAURIE:
"Little boy! Little boy! Come here!"

The little boy just stood there looking
around. LAURIE then ran outside and
scooped him up and ran back to the
police station. She put him down and
then turned around shutting and locking
the doors. She then turned to the little
boy.

LAURIE:
"Are you ok? Are you hurt?"

She looked and saw that he was bleeding
on his arm. She saw that it was a bite
mark. She ran and grabbed the first aid
kit and opened it up. She began to patch
up his arm. She then looked at his his
face and noticed it was staring blankly.

LAURIE:
"Hey, are you ok? Stay with me."

She turned her head for once second and
the little boy jumped up biting her in
the neck and took a huge chunk out!

BUB'S' PUB/NIGHTFALL:

SETH was unlocking a back door.

MIKHAIL:
"Where's this lead to?"

SETH:
"An alleyway behind a couple of the
stores."

They opened the door and began to walk
out. They slowly made their down the
alleyway. They heard all the screaming
and the WAITRESS began to cry. MIKHAIL
stopped and looked at her.

MIKHAIL:
"Hey, hey, it's gonna be alright."

WAITRESS:
"What's going on?"

MIKHAIL:
"I don't know. But were gonna be ok. We
need to get somewhere safe."

SETH:
"Come on guys we gotta wrap this up."

MIKHAIL:
"Anywhere to go?"

SETH:
"Police Station. My brother works there,
plus they might have an idea of what's
going on."

Some ZOMBIES were following them from
the bar.

MIKHAIL:
"Shit."

They began to run. They bumped into the
MERCER family. MIKHAIL bumped into ERIC
knocking him down.

ERIC:
"Watch where the fuck you're going!"

He got back up and stood face to face
with MIKHAIL.

MIKHAIL:
"Come on, we need to go, you'll be safer
with us."

BUFFY:
"Where?"

MIKHAIL:
"I don't know. Anywhere but here."

ERIC:
"Well that's just fucking great."

SETH:
"We're heading to the police station."

MIKHAIL:
"Look out here were sitting ducks. We
need to go now."

Then they heard some voices in the
distance. They looked and saw JAMES from
DV-MART. He was standing at the back
door.

JAMES:
"Come on, in here!"

They ran to the door with ZOMBIES hot on
their trail. SETH began shooting them
with the SHERIFF"S gun. None them were
head shots. They made it to he door and
all rushed in. ERIC pushed the WAITRESS
out of his way and she fell down.
MIKHAIL saw her but couldn't make it in
time. Three ZOMBIES attacked her. She
screamed and MIKHAIL just stood there.
SETH walked up to him.

SETH:
"Come on, we gotta go."

They both walked into the store and
slammed the door shut.

<u>**DINOSAUR VALLEY/NIGHTTIME:**</u>

Bodies were littered all over the
streets. People were running and
screaming. Within an hour everyone in the
entire valley had been killed. It was a
massacre in DINOSAUR VALLEY. Then it was
quiet
soon. All that was heard was the ZOMBIES
shuffling around aimlessly.

<u>**CHAPTER 5**</u>:

<u>**DINOSAUR VALLEY/EARLY AFTERNOON**</u>:

CRASH! A police patrol car came crashing through the woods. Inside was ASH. He was still alive. There were a bunch of ZOMBIES on his car. He was driving like a mad man trying to shake them off. Then a ZOMBIE put is hand through the side window and grabbed ASH'S throat. ASH began to choke, he then slammed on his breaks. All the ZOMBIES flew off the car. ASH sighed as the ZOMBIE that had his throat loosened its grip. ASH then looked and saw just an arm. When he hit the breaks the ZOMBIE'S arm must have been separated from its body. Then suddenly the hand began to move again. ASH grabbed it and through it out the window. He got out and found himself behind DV-Mart. He grabbed a bag out of the car then he shot the ZOMBIE'S on the ground. He approached the back door. He went to open it but it was locked.

ASH:
"Shit."

He turned around towards the ZOMBIES. He then looked back at the lock.

ASH:
"Fuck it."

He shot the lock and ran inside shutting the door behind him. He leaned up against the door giving another sigh of relief.

Realizing that he just shot off the lock,
he had to find something to barricade
the door. He looked around and reached
for a chair. He turned around and saw a
hand stuck in the door. It was still
moving. He shook his head in disbelief.
Then he placed the chair next to the
door. He then held his gun high
searching to see if it was safe.

ASH:
"Hello?"

There was no answer. He continued to
walk around. Listening to the ZOMBIES
banging on the doors trying to get in.
Ash walked past a mannequin. He headed
to the main office in hopes to find a
phone. All of a sudden he was attacked.
The mannequin who wasn't a mannequin at
all but a ZOMBIE. ASH and the ZOMBIE
both fell back. The ZOMBIE began
chomping his teeth at ASH. ASH grabbed
the ZOMBIE by the hair. He pulled it
back and threw it. He got up and shot
the ZOMBIE in the head. Brain and blood
flew all over the place. ASH quickly
headed to the office door. When he did
he found it locked.

ASH:
"Come on! Doesn't anyone keep anything
unlocked!"

He kicked the door in. When it flew open
he hit someone. There was a yell. ASH
lifted his gun up again. He pointed it,
looked and saw some people in the
office.

ASH:
"What the hell is going on?"

The people in the office were ERIC,
BUFFY, SARAH, MIKHAIL, and the two
DV-Mart workers JAMES, and STEPHANIE.
ASH saw SETH and gave a sigh of relief.

SETH:
"Ash, you're alive?"

ASH:
"You ok?"

SETH:
"Yeah, I was worried."

They embraced in a quick hug and then
ASH broke away.

ASH:
"What the fuck you couldn't help me? I
shouted out, and no one answered."

ERIC:
"Well excuse me, but none of us have x-
ray vision. And besides it could have
been those things out there."

ASH:
"Who the hell are you?"

ERIC:
"I'm Eric Mercer, and you are?"

ASH:
"Name's Ash Redfield. I'm the deputy of
this Valley."

ERIC:
"Doesn't look that way to me."

SETH:
"Where have you been?"

ASH:
"I was out on call. Then I was attacked
by some of those things. What happened
here? What's wrong with those people?"

SETH:
"No one knows. They came out of nowhere.
Sheriff Hooper's dead."

ASH:
"What?"

SETH:
"We tried to make it to the police
station but there were to many of those
things out there so me ended up in here.
By the time anyone knew what was going
on it was too late. All of us ran and
made it here and hid in the office away
from the windows. We were waiting
for help until you showed up."

ERIC:
"Yeah, I think help should be here soon."

ASH:
"I don't think we should wait."

ERIC:
"What do you mean?"

ASH:
"I think we should get off the island,
get a hold of the Army, Marines, Air
force the whole enchilada; I'm in way
over my head."

ERIC:
"No, I think we should stay put."

ASH:
"We'll I don't give a damn what you
think. I'm the law so I'm in charge."

ERIC:
"There's too many of those things out
there, anyway."

ASH:
"Exactly, that's why we should get out
of here, before anymore of those things
know we're in here."

BUFFY:
"I think we need to leave. "

ERIC got mad when BUFFY agreed with ASH.

ERIC:
"No, we're staying right here. Someone
will show up."

ASH:
"And what if they don't? Are you willing
to take that chance,
because I'm not. Not until I know all
the options."

ERIC:
"What fucking options? And who the fuck
gave you the right to decide for the
rest of us?"

ASH began to get sick of arguing with
ERIC.

ASH:
"This badge asshole. And if you don't
have any options then please
do me and humanity a favor by shutting
the fuck up."

BUFFY:
"We came on the ferry. Can't we just
take it back?"

ASH:
"Yeah, but I'm not even sure it's still
there. It could be back at the main
land."

MIKHAIL:
"Well we can always take my boat. Shit
we can all fit."

STEPHANIE:
"Really?"

MIKHAIL:
"Yeah, we can get in a car and drive up
to the marina."

ASH:
"Yeah, but what car can fit eight
people?"

MIKHAIL:
"A van?"

BUFFY:
"Ours is down the street?"

ASH:
"Yeah?"

BUFFY:
"Yeah, we can walk down to it, but what
about Sarah?"

ERIC:
"She's not going anywhere."

SARAH:
"I'll be fine, daddy."

SETH:
"What about weapons?"

ASH:
"We could always hit the station before
we leave. This way we could arm
ourselves. It'll give us more of a
chance."

SETH:
"Alright, sounds like a plan to me."

ASH:
"Then it's settled, we walk. But not now
there's too many of them. Let's get just
relax and maybe with some luck they'll
leave when they realize they can't get
in."

DV-MART/MAIN OFFICE: NIGHTTIME

ASH was upstairs looking out the window.
Then SARAH entered the room.

SARAH:
"You know my father thinks you're gonna
get us killed."

ASH:
"I really don't care what you're father
thinks of me, kid."

SARAH:
"My names SARAH, not kid."

ASH:
"Sarah, I'm officer Redfield, but you
can call me Ash."

He smiled at her. She smiled back.

ASH:
"I've never seen you guys here before,
you move here?"

SARAH:
"Yeah, my dad got a new job here."

ASH:
"Where'd you come from?"

SARAH:
"We moved here from Santa Barbara."
(Sighs)
"I wanna go home."

She walked up and sat right next to ASH.

ASH:
"We'll you might be going back sooner
than you think."

SARAH:
"I hope so, I hate this place."

ASH:
"We'll it used to be really peaceful,
until last night."

BUFFY entered the room.

BUFFY:
"There you are honey. I've been looking
for you."

BUFFY took SARAH into her arms.

BUFFY:
"I don't want you running off like that.
With everything that is going on, I need
to know where you are at all times."

SARAH:
"I was here with officer Redfield, I
think I'll be fine mom."

BUFFY:
"Go to your father and get some sleep."

SARAH:
"Fine."

Sighing she walked out of the room.
BUFFY stayed with ASH. She walked up to
the window and glanced outside.

ASH:
"Cute kid."

BUFFY:
"She can be a handful at times though."

ASH:
"Most kids can be."

BUFFY:
"Do you have any?"

ASH:
"No, I don't have the time. My job comes
first."

BUFFY:
"So there's no Mrs. Redfield?"

ASH:
"No. Well almost.

BUFFY:
"What happened? If you don't mind me
asking?"

ASH was surprised to see her show any
interest. Especially during a time like
this.

ASH:
"Just two different worlds. Didn't work
out, that's all.

BUFFY:
"What was her name?"

ASH:
"Diana Ortiz."

BUFFY:
"She must have been a lucky lady."

ASH stopped talking and looked back out
the window. BUFFY stood there and
realized he didn't want to talk about it
anymore.

BUFFY:
"How is it outside?"

ASH:
(Looking Out The Window)
"They don't know we're in here yet, but
I don't know how long it will last."
(Looking At BUFFY)
"I heard you're husband doesn't like
me."

BUFFY:
"Who Eric?"
(Rolling Her Eyes)
"He doesn't like anyone. He thinks he's
holier than thow."

ASH:
"Well he needs a reality check lady, this
is my valley and everyone here is my
responsibility. That includes your
family. So Eric is either going to
listen to me, or he can go his own way."

BUFFY:
"We'll he can be very stubborn when he
doesn't get his way."

ASH:
"Can I ask a question?"

BUFFY:
(Hesitant)
"Sure, ask away."

ASH:
"Why is he such a dick?"

BUFFY:
"Hey, he may be a dick but he's still my husband."

ASH:
(Sarcastically)
"Sorry."

BUFFY:
(Pausing)
"Well, seeing as we might not make it out of this alive….

ASH:
(Chuckling)
"Thanks, much faith."

BUFFY:
"Oh come on, we don't know what's going to happen here and you know it."

ASH:
"You were saying."

BUFFY:
"Well, Sarah wasn't supposed to happen."

ASH:
"What do you mean?"

BUFFY:
"Well she was an accident, we were young
and in love, and had our whole life ahead
of us, I guess he's upset cause he never
got to live the life he always wanted."

ASH rolled his eyes and let out an
annoying sigh.

ASH:
"This story, come on lady.

No offense but I hear shit like this all
the time."

BUFFY:
"What story?"

ASH:
"The whole poor me routine. Everyone's
got a story, and I'm really sick of
hearing them."

BUFFY couldn't believe what she heard.
This was coming from a man
of the law.

BUFFY:
"What about you, huh? What's your story?"

ASH paused for a moment.

ASH:
"I don't have one, Nothing bad ever
happened to me."

BUFFY knew he was hiding something.

BUFFY:
"I don't think that's true."

She kept prying which caused ASH to
snap.

ASH:
"Ok fine, shall I tell you? I mean do
you think that you're the only one with
problems? Do you want to know how I
served my country only to get left
behind during a mission? Or how when I
was captured the people there beat and
tortured me for 2 years?"

BUFFY:
"I'm sorry, I didn't mean too."

ASH got even more upset.

ASH:
"But of course your did! Do you also
want to know that because everyone
thought I was dead, my fiance, the love
of my life left me? She didn't even hold
on to hope! She just up and moved away.
Then when I was found and declared
alive, I still haven't heard from her.
It's been over five years! So please
spare me the poor me routine. I mean I
don't know if you realize but the whole
world is basically coming to an end and
I don't even know if I can help us!"

BUFFY stood there for a few minutes in
shock and silence

ASH:
"And remember, just when you think you
have it tough. Someone else was it
worse!"

BUFFY couldn't listen anymore and
angrily walked away. ASH looked at her
leaving. He stood there and realized how
much of an asshole he had been. He
walked up and lightly grabbed her hand.
She pulled away from him.

ASH:
"Hey, hey. Listen, I'm really sorry. I
was out of line, I apologize."

BUFFY:
"I get this all the time from my
husband. I don't need it from anyone
else. I'm sorry you went through hell, I
really am. But it's hell of other people
too."

ASH went to put his hand on BUFFY'S face
but she pulled back and flinched out of
fear. It was at that moment ASH realized
BUFFY was abused by ERIC. He put his
hand back on her face and she accepted
it this time. She knew no matter how
upset he got, she was safe with him.
They looked into each others eyes. BUFFY
then sighed, then sat down.

BUFFY:
"You know when she was born it wasn't
just the two of us anymore. Then
everything changed and he started
drinking…"

ASH:
"He doesn't hit you guys does he?"

He knew ERIC hit her, he just wanted to hear her say it. Thinking maybe it would help to talk about it.

BUFFY:
"Not Sarah, I provoke him so he focuses his anger on me instead of her. And besides it doesn't hurt as much anymore. I think maybe if I keep my mouth shut he wouldn't get so angry."

He walked up to her, kneeling down and put his hands on her face.

ASH:
"Hey, you shouldn't keep your mouth shut, if you gotta say something then say it. Don't be afraid."

BUFFY:
"But if I stay quiet…."

She paused and pulled back from him.

BUFFY:
"I don't know why I'm telling you this. . . . never mind ."

ASH saw tears coming down her face.

ASH:
"It's not your fault, no one deserves to be treated like that."

She began to wipe away the tears.

BUFFY:
"Thanks, but I'd better get back before
he comes looking for me."

ASH:
"Ok. If you ever wanna talk."

BUFFY:
"Thanks, but I'll be fine."

She began to walk out and then stopped.

BUFFY:
"You should get some sleep."

ASH:
"There's no sleep in my job."

BUFFY:
"We're gonna need you at one hundred
percent to get us outta her tomorrow."

ASH smirked.

ASH:
"So now you have faith, lady?"

BUFFY:
"My name is Buffy."

ASH:
"Ok, Buffy. I'll get some sleep."

She smiled at him. He smiled back. She
walked out. ASH looked back out the
window and noticed lights out in the
distance.

They looked like road flares.
He then looked down and saw the ZOMBIES
walking away and heading towards the
flares.

CHAPTER 6:

DV-MART/MAIN ENTRANCE: MORNING

There were no signs of the ZOMBIES anywhere in front of the back door.

ASH:
"It looks clear, how far up the street is your van?"

BUFFY:
"Not far."

ASH:
"We'll everyone stay behind me and don't wander off. We're going to stay on the side of the buildings until I tell you further, got it."

They all nodded.

ERIC:
"This is bullshit, we are never going to make it."

ASH:
"Keep your mouth shut and don't open it again unless you got something positive to say."

SETH:
"What about the police station? Do you think we should get weapons first then head for the car?"

MIKHAIL:
"Which one is closer?"

ASH looked at ERIC and BUFFY.

ASH:
"Where is your van parked?"

ERIC:
"It's in the middle of the road, next to
a gas station."

ASH:
"Damn."

BUFFY looked concerned.

BUFFY:
"Is that bad?"

ASH:
"It's closer than the police station."

ERIC:
"So? We get in the car and head to the
station. What's the big deal."

SETH:
"You're car is that way. The police
station is in the opposite direction."

ASH:
"He's right, we'd be back tracking. I
say we get to the van and get out of
here as soon as we can. We don't know
how far this thing has spread."

BUFFY:
"What do you mean? Spread? Like a virus?"

ASH:
"It's a possibility. I mean I've never
seen anything like this before. People
acting that. It might be an airborne
virus or it could be something in the
water."

ERIC:
"So that means it could be anywhere?"

ASH:
"Yes, or it could just be here on the
island, it could be the whole world for
all we know."

ASH then looked at MIKHAIL and SETH. He
handed them both a gun each.

ASH:
"Be careful, it may be small but it has
a powerful kick, and make sure the
safety's off."

MIKHAIL:
"I own a gun, I know how to work one."

ERIC:
"Why don't I get a gun?"

ASH:
"Because you have a temper and we don't
need you going off half cocked ready to
save the world."

ERIC:
"This is. . . ."

ASH then pointed his gun towards ERIC.

ASH:
"What did I say? If you don't have anything positive to say, don't say anything at all."(Pause) "Didn't your mother teach you anything?"

ERIC went to open his mouth and ASH put up his finger. ERIC quickly shut up. BUFFY turned around to hold back a smirk. ASH then looked at SARAH.

ASH:
"Ok Sarah, I need you to be my shadow, keep your eyes on me ok, and only me, got that."

SARAH:
(Nervous)
"Ok."

ASH opened the back door. He looked and saw no ZOMBIES.

ASH:
"Let's go."

DV-MART ALLEY WAY/MORNING:

They all walked out and followed ASH. It was eerily quiet. It just the sounds of moaning in the distance. As they were walking STEPHANIE looked over. She couldn't believe what she saw. It was the body of a dead woman laying on the ground. On her finger was a large diamond ring. STEPHANIE walked away from the group and up to the dead body.

She took the ring off the dead woman's finger and smiled.

STEPHANIE:
"Come to mamma."

She kissed the ring and began to make her way back towards the others. As she did the dead girls eyes opened, she grabbed STEPHANIE by the arm. When STEPHANIE turned around she saw the dead woman wasn't dead anymore. STEPHANIE saw that she was a ZOMBIE and screamed. The ZOMBIE woman bit STEPHANIE in the mouth. With one bite ripped out her tongue and pulled off her lips. ASH and the others heard STEPHANIE'S screams and so did the ZOMBIES. JAMES saw and became completely enraged.

He took SETH'S gun and began to fire at the ZOMBIES.

JAMES:
"You bastards!"

JAMES walked closer as he shot at the woman. But instead he was hitting a pick up truck that was behind her. ASH noticed that he was hitting close to the gas tank.

ASH:
"Hey, stop!"

He didn't listen.

ASH:
"Everybody get down!"

JAMES fired one more shot, it hit the
tank. "BOOM!" The truck exploded and
everyone went flying. MIKHAIL flew back
and hit a car. ERIC and BUFFY ducked
while SETH protected SARAH. JAMES flew
back and the gun flew out of his hand.
After a few seconds ASH looked up. He
saw the ZOMBIES heading their way.

ASH:
"Run!"

ASH got up and ran towards JAMES. He
picking the gun up and tossed it at
SETH. He grabbed JAMES and started to
lift him off the ground.

ASH:
"Come on get up!"

JAMES:
"No! Just go leave me here I can't
walk."

ASH looked down at JAMES'S leg. There
was a large gash, with his tissue and
bone

showing. ASH then looked at JAMES.

ASH:
"No, I'm not leaving you behind! Get up
now!"

MIKHAIL:
"We need to get out of here!"

ASH picked JAMES up placing his arm
around his neck.

They ran as fast as they could with JAMES
limping. SETH noticed a door behind a
dumpster.

SETH:
"Guys this way!"

They all began to head to the door.
Suddenly a sewer top flew up and a
ZOMBIE came out. It grabbed SARAH by the
leg and tripped her.

SARAH:
"MOM!"

BUFFY turned around, seeing her daughter
in danger.

BUFFY:
"Sarah!"

She ran to her aid, but ERIC held her
back

ERIC:
"Forget her, she's just a kid!"

The ZOMBIE bit SARAH in the leg, SARAH
screamed loudly in pain! ASH tossed
JAMES to SETH. He ran to SARAH'S aid
kicking the ZOMBIE in the head, like it
was a soccer ball. The ZOMBIE fell back
into the sewer. ASH picked SARAH up and
began to run with her. Then a ZOMBIE ran
and jumped up off of a car. ASH spun
around seeing the ZOMBIE heading
straight at him and SARAH. He closed his
eyes and tried to protect SARAH.....
BLAM!

He opened his eyes and saw the ZOMBIE
fly back. He looked over and saw
MIKHAIL. Then SETH shouted to them.

SETH:
"Come on, we found a place."

ASH and MIKHAIL ran up to the door.

ASH:
"I owe you one."

MIKHAIL nodded. Then kicked in the door
and all ran inside.

<u>LUCIO'S APIZZA/MORNING:</u>

SETH placed JAMES down and helped
MIKHAIL shut and block the door. BUFFY
ran to ASH and SARAH. She took SARAH out
of ASH'S arms.

BUFFY:
(In tears)
"Thank you. Oh, my God. Thank you.

Out of breath ASH nodded. BUFFY walked
away with SARAH. ASH looked up at JAMES
and grabbed him. ASH threw him back
against the wall.

ASH:
"What the fuck it wrong with you! You
could've killed us. What the fuck were
you thinking!"

JAMES:
(Scared)
"I don't know, I'm sorry. I wasn't
thinking."

ASH threw him back. Then walked up to
SARAH and BUFFY.

ASH:
"What happened?"

BUFFY:
"It bit her in the leg."

ASH looked at it. A piece of skin was
missing.

ASH:
"Shit, it looks bad. We need to clean in
now. Guys look around and see where we
are."

SETH and MIKHAIL looked around. ERIC
walked up to BUFFY and SARAH.

ERIC:
"She'll be ok."

BUFFY:
(Aggravated)
"Get away from me."

ERIC went to put his hand on her
shoulder. But she shrugged it away.

BUFFY:
"Don't touch me."

ERIC rolled his eyes and walked away.

ERIC:
"Whatever."

SETH and MIKHAIL were in a kitchen area.
There was a mess in the main floor area.
Blood splattered all over the place with
chairs knocked over. You could tell
people tried to get out in a hurry.

SETH:
"I think we're in Luico's?"

MIKHAIL:
"The pizza place?"

SETH:
"At least we won't go hungry."

SETH went up and checked the door to
make sure it was locked and steady. ERIC
looked around and couldn't believe where
they were.

ERIC:
"Nice place. Our Alamo."

SETH:
"Shut up, like I fucking knew."

ASH:
"Shut up Eric, I don't wanna here
another word out of you."

MIKHAIL came up with a table cloth and
handed it to ASH. ASH tore it in half.
Then began to wrap it around SARAH'S
leg.

BUFFY:
(In Tears)
"Do you think it will work?"

ASH:
(Unsure)
"It should for now."

SARAH was passed out. ASH then took the
other half of the table cloth to JAMES.
He began to wrap the gash on his leg up.

JAMES:
"We need to get out of here?"

ASH:
"No way, cause of you it's too dangerous
to go outside right now. We'll have to
hold up in here for a while."

They all sat down to catch their breath.
JAMES then began a little prayer.
MIKHAIL walked passes him. He looked at
JAMES, who's hand were folded in a
prayer.

MIKHAIL:
"Save your prayers boy. God doesn't live
here anymore."

LUCIO'S APIZZA ROOFTOP/NIGHTTIME:

ASH was once again on watching down at
the ZOMBIES. BUFFY came up.

BUFFY:
"Hey, how does it look out there?"

She walked up next to ASH at the edge
and looked down.

ASH:
"It looks pretty good."

Again ASH looked into the distance again
and saw more road flares. This time
there were lights flashing as well.
He looked down and saw the ZOMBIES
heading in that direction again.

ASH:
"I just wish I knew what the hell was
going on?"

BUFFY:
"Eric thinks it's a virus or plague."

ASH:
"I really don't care what that asshole
thinks, I know he's your husband but I
can't stand the guy."

Then there was silence and BUFFY began to
walk away. She then stopped.

BUFFY:
"I just wanted to say thank you for
earlier. For saving Sarah."

ASH:
"Don't worry about it. It's my job."

BUFFY:
(Breaking Down)
"If you hadn't helped her. God knows
what would have happened?"

ASH:
"Well I have a feeling he's not
listening right now."

BUFFY showed a little smile.

ASH:
"How is she?"

BUFFY:
"She has a slight fever, but otherwise
she's doing fine. She's down with Eric
right now."

ASH walked up to her.

ASH:
"Don't worry, we'll get her to a
doctor."

BUFFY:
"You promise?"

He slowly grabbed her hand.

ASH:
"Yeah, I promise."

BUFFY began to breakdown and cry.

ASH:
"Hey, hey."

ASH then began to hold her. The put his
hand under her chin, lifting it up.

ASH:
"It's going to be ok?"

BUFFY:
"I can't loose her, I just can't. If
something happens to her…."

BUFFY then rested her head on ASH'S
chest.

ASH:
"Don't talk like that. She'll be fine."

Then ERIC popped his head up and saw
BUFFY with ASH. HE coughed loudly to get
their attention. ASH and BUFFY turned
around and saw ERIC. Her and ASH then
separated.

ERIC:
"Buffy, Sarah wants you."

BUFFY:
"Ok."

She headed to the ladder and looked back
at ASH.

BUFFY:
"Bye."

Then she left with ERIC.

LUCIO'S APIZZA STORAGE/NIGHTTIME:

When they got down ERIC stopped BUFFY.

ERIC:
"What was that?"

BUFFY:
"What was what?"

ERIC:
(Raising His Voice)
"You and that prick!"

BUFFY:
"What are you talking about?"

ERIC:
"You hanging all over him like that."

BUFFY:
"I wasn't hanging all over him, I
started to think of Sarah. I'm worried
about her, I just needed someone to talk
too, Eric."

ERIC:
"You couldn't talk to me, you had to go
into the arms of another man."

BUFFY:
"Eric, I didn't....." (Pausing For
Moment) "You know what I'm not getting
into it right now."

She walked away. ERIC grabbed her arm.

ERIC:
"Yes you are."

He tightened his grip.

BUFFY:
"Eric please."

ERIC:
"I catch you with him again, I swear
I'll….."

She pulled away and got straight in
ERIC'S face.

BUFFY:
"You'll what! That is your daughter in
there, and if you were even half a man
then you would have been there for her
instead of hiding, then she wouldn't
have gotten attacked."

ERIC:
"What do you want from me! She's just a
fucking kid!"

BUFFY'S eyes widened with tears. She was
in complete shock. She could not believe
what he had just said! Just a kid. Their
daughter is just a kid!

BUFFY:
"You're right. You're absolutely fucking
right! She's just a fucking kid. Now if
you don't mind that fucking kid needs
me."

With tears in her eyes, she stormed away
from ERIC, who just stood there in
complete shock.

ERIC:
"Buffy don't you walk away from me!
Buffy!"

She slammed the door on him. ERIC stood
there all alone.

CHAPTER 7:

LUCIOS'APIZZA MAIN OFFICE/LATE MORNING:

It had been a few days and everyone was
all sitting around trying
to stay hidden.

ASH:
"Well they're pretty separated out
there, but I wouldn't chance going to
the van just yet."

BUFFY:
"We've gotta do something now, her
fevers getting worse."

ASH:
"We will, Buffy. Nothing's gonna
happen."

ASH walked away. SETH followed.

SETH:
"What's up?"

ASH:
"We gotta do something, but I don't know
what. She needs medical attention and
all we have here is sauce and
pepperoni."

SETH:
"Hard to believe a place like this has
no first aid kit?"

SETH sat there for one second and
thought. Then it hit him.

SETH:
"King's gas station might have
something?"

ASH:
"Yeah, but how far is it?"

SETH:
"Two buildings down."

ASH:
"Ok, I'll go."

They met up with the others.

ASH:
"There's a gas station up the street I'm
gonna go to it and get some supplies for
Sarah, then bring the van around."

BUFFY:
"No, you need to stay here in case those
things get in."

MIKHAIL:
"She's right. You stay, I'm quieter so
I'll go."

MIKHAIL tossed a set of keys at ASH.

MIKHAIL:
"Here, my boats called the Argento."

ERIC:
"I'm coming too. She's my daughter."

BUFFY:
"Eric."

She was confused. His selfish ass never
volunteers for anything. Now suddenly he
wants to play hero?

ERIC:
"Buffy, I'll be fine."

He kissed her on the head. Then walked
up to MIKHAIL.

ERIC:
"You ready?"

ASH:
"Be careful."

He looked at MIKHAIL.

ASH:
"And watch your back."

He gave MIKHAIL one of the guns.

DINOSAUR VALLEY STREETS/LATE MORNING:

They stayed hidden behind the cars and
the big oil tanker truck.

KING'S GAS STATION/LATE MORNING:

They made it to the gas station and went
inside.

MIKHAIL:
"Ok look around of anything useful."

ERIC rolled his eyes and began to look.

After searching for a while MIKHAIL
found some rubbing alcohol. ERIC grabbed
some cotton balls and some wraps.

ERIC:
"You think we should grab anything
else?"

MIKHAIL:
"Like what?"

ERIC:
"Water, weapons?"

MIKHAIL:
"Weapons?"

ERIC:
"It's a gas station? They might have a
gun under the counter?"

MIKHAIL:
"This is a peaceful valley not the
Bronx."

ERIC:
"Just do it."

MIKHAIL went behind the counter looking
for a gun. He couldn't believe what he
saw. His eyes lit up like a kid at
Christmas.

MIKHAIL:
"I don't believe it!"

ERIC:
"What? Is it a gun?"

MIKHAIL:
"No better."

He pulled out a small box of cigars.

ERIC:
"Cigars?"

He grabbed one and sniffed it.

MIKHAIL:
"Not just cigars, Cubans."

MIKHAIL stuffed them in to his pocket
with a huge smile on his face. Then he
walked up to the door with ERIC. They
saw that there were more ZOMBIES
outside. They were dragging a body and
tearing it apart. Blood and guts flew
everywhere. ERIC shook his head. MIKHAIL
lit up a cigar.

MIKHAIL:
"Ok so now how do we get back?"

ERIC:
"Well it seems the only way to stop
them is to give them what they want?"

MIKHAIL:
"So what do we give them?"

ERIC:
"Give me your gun."

MIKHAIL handed it to ERIC. BLAM! ERIC
shot MIKHAIL in the leg and MIKHAIL
shouted. ERIC ran to the back of the
gas station.

MIKHAIL:
"Fuck! You bastard!"

ERIC then shot the glass door. The
ZOMBIES heard the noise and headed to
the gas station.

ERIC:
"See ya."

ERIC ran out the door shutting it behind
him.

MIKHAIL:
"Nyet! I'm gonna fucking kill you!"

He began to crawl off as the ZOMBIES
came pouring in the gas station.

DINOSAUR VALLEY STREET/LATE MORNING:

ERIC ran up to his van and started it
up. He drove it to LUCIO'S, got out and
banged on the door.

ERIC:
"Let me in!"

ASH opened the door. ERIC ran in.

LUCIOS'S APIZZA/NIGHTTIME:

ASH looked around and didn't see MIKHAIL.

ERIC:
"Shut the door!"

ASH shut and bolted the door.

ERIC stood there out of breath.

ASH:
"Where's Mikhail?"

ERIC:
"He didn't make it. Those thing fucking
ate him."

ASH:
"You saw it!"

ERIC:
"Of course I fucking saw it! They move
so fast."

ASH:
"You got the car though?"

ERIC:
"Yeah it's outside. There should be
enough gas to get to the marina."

ASH:
"Well we can't go now they're all over
the place."

ERIC:
"Then we wait again. They'll leave."

SETH:
"We heard the gun shots."

ERIC:
"It was the Russian."

SETH:
"Mikhail."

He corrected him and was upset with the
lack of respect.

ERIC:
"He shot them while I got the van. By
the time I turned around they were all
over him."

SETH:
"I bet."

SETH had a hard time believing the
story.

ERIC:
"What are you trying to say?"

SETH:
"Nothing."

ERIC approached SETH and got into his
face. ASH jumped in front of them.

ASH:
"Enough. There's a lot going on right
now and we don't need this shit."

ERIC stared SETH down, then gave him a
smirk. He then walked way towards up to
BUFFY and SARAH. SETH stared at ASH.

SETH:
"You buy that?"

ASH:
"I'm not sure. It does sound a little
off. We'll just have to keep an eye on
him."

<u>**CHAPTER 8:**</u>

<u>**LUCIO'S APIZZA ROOFTOP/NIGHTTIME:**</u>

ASH and SETH were looking down.

There were even more ZOMBIES than
before.

ASH:
"These fuckers just keep coming!"

SETH:
"I know. Don't they have homes or
something?"

It got quiet for a moment as they stood
there. SETH then broke the silence.

SETH:
"Do you think were gonna make it?"

ASH:
"I guarantee it."

SETH was surprised to hear his brother
so hopeful.

SETH:
"How can you be sure?"

ASH:
"Because I'm not gonna give up until we
are all safely on that boat on headed to
the main land."

SETH:
"What do you think caused all of this?"

ASH:
"I'm not sure, but I've been thinking
Old Man Lombardi said something to me a
few nights ago."

SETH:
"What?"

ASH:
"He said he saw something fall from the
sky in Prospect. And that's where I was
when I was attacked, and that's the same
night all this shit went down."

SETH:
"Or that old priest was right, and it
could be the judgment day."

They both laughed, but ASH stopped when
he saw the same flares and lights again.

SETH:
"What? What is it?"

ASH:
"I keep seeing those lights. All week,
there those flares and lights.

Almost like vehicles."

SETH:
"I wonder why?"

ASH:
"I don't know, but the flares attract
these things."

ASH looked down and showed SETH.

ASH:
"See? Look how they follow. Like some
sort of distraction."

The ZOMBIES started to follow the
flares.

SETH:
"So you think that...."

Then there was a loud scream from down
stairs. ASH and SETH rushed down the
ladder.

LUCIO'S APIZZA MAIN OFFICE/NIGHTTIME:

They ran into the office room.

ASH:
"What's wrong?"

BUFFY:
"It's Sarah. She's not breathing."

ASH put his gun on the table approached
her body and looked at her. He felt for
her pulse and didn't get a response. He
then tried to give CPR, but again there
was no response.

ASH:
"Come on kid."

BUFFY:
"Keep trying, please!"

ASH kept trying but was getting nothing.
SARAH was gone. ASH looked up at ERIC
and BUFFY.

ASH:
"I'm sorry."

BUFFY:
"No, no, no, no!"

She began break down. ERIC just lost it.
BUFFY went to SARAH'S body and began to
cry uncontrollably. ERIC walked up to
BUFFY. He grabbed her by the arm yanking
her up, causing SARAH'S lifeless body
to hit the floor.

ERIC:
"This is your fault!"

BUFFY:
"My fault, how is this my fault!"

ERIC:
"You should have been watching her! If
she was by your side she wouldn't have
been attacked!"

BUFFY:
"You're the one who wanted to come to
this god damn island!"

ASH put his hand on ERIC's back.

ASH:
"You both need to calm down."

ERIC:
"No you calm down!" (Throwing ASH's Hand
Back) "I just lost my daughter so fuck
you!"

He looked over to BUFFY with disgust on
his face.

ERIC:
"And you, you're fucking useless! We
should've stayed put but nooooooo, you
wanted to fucking listen to this fucking
jerk!"

He pointed at ASH. SMACK! He hit BUFFY
across the face knocking her down. WHAM!
ASH then punched ERIC in his mouth. ERIC
fell back against the wall.

ASH:
"Don't you ever put your hands on her
again."

ERIC got back up and tried to punch ASH.
ASH blocked and hit ERIC right in the
throat. ERIC fell down again. ASH walked
up to BUFFY.

ASH:
"You ok?"

He extended his hand out to her but she
looked away from him with her hand
covering her face.

BUFFY:
"Yeah, it's nothing he's hit me harder."

ERIC pulled his gun and pointed it at
ASH.

BUFFY:
"Look out!"

With lighting quick reflexes ASH pulled
out his knife. Both he and ERIC were in
a stare down. ERIC had the gun at ASH'S
neck. ASH had the knife at ERIC'S throat.

ASH:
"Go ahead Eric, just give me the excuse.
Please."

SETH:
"Especially since you killed Mikhail."

ERIC looked surprised at this claim.

ERIC:
"I don't know what you're fucking
talking about. I told you he was killed
by those things."

SETH:
"Yes, you said that he died killing
them."

ERIC started to get nervous..

ERIC:
"That's true."

SETH:
"Then how come you have his gun?"

ERIC looked at both of them and unlocked
his safety.

ERIC:
"I'm getting out of here and I'm taking
Buffy with me."

ASH:
"You can go, but she's staying right
here."

ERIC:
"She's my wife."

As they were arguing SARAH'S eyes opened
up. BUFFY and SETH looked on. Then SARAH
jumped on ERIC, biting him in the neck.
She pulled out a chunk of flesh. He
shouted and threw her back. She hit the
wall and jumped back up. ERIC ran out of
the room and SARAH attacked ASH. They
both fell back and she tried to bite
him. JAMES stumbled up and tried to
pulled her off of ASH, she turned around
and bit JAMES on the arm. ASH rolled
over grabbing is gun. SARAH ran toward
BUFFY and SETH.

ASH:
"Hey!"

SARAH stopped and looked at ASH. Then
she shrieked really loudly. She ran
toward ASH and he shot her directly in
the head. BLAM! Her blood flew on BUFFY
and SETH. BUFFY then went hysterical, it
was a mixed reaction of crying and
screaming,JAMES was holding his arm. He
was shocked and disgusted.

JAMES:
"Fuck! Fuck! Did you see that? Goddamn!
She took a chunk right out
of my fucking arm!"

ASH:
"We need to clean that up right now.
Seth get a towel."

SETH:
"Got it."

ASH:
"Eric get some alcohol."

There was no response from ERIC.

ASH:
"Eric? Eric where the fuck are you?"

Then they heard a car start. ASH and
SETH looked at each other.

ASH/SETH:
"The Van!"

LUCIO'S APIZZA ROOFTOP/NIGHTTIME:

They looked down of the roof. ERIC had
taken their escape vehicle
and began to drive off with it.

ASH:
"I'm gonna fucking kill him!"

ERIC tried to drive through the ZOMBIES.
There were too many of them. They
covered the van. ERIC couldn't see where
he was going. He crashed it in to the
parked fuel tanker across the street.
ERIC, the van, the fuel tanker, and the
ZOMBIES were all incinerated in
the explosion.

SETH:
"Now what are we gonna do?"

ASH then looked at SETH.

ASH:
"The back door?"

They both headed back down the ladder.

<u>LUCIO'S APIZZA MAIN OFFICE/NITGHTIME</u>:

JAMES holding the door.

ASH:
"What's going on?"

JAMES:
"They got in!"

ASH:
"Shit!"

ASH then grabbed the couch with SETH.
They both pushed it in front
of the door.

SETH:
"There's no way that's gonna keep them
back."

The ZOMBIES began to break down the door.

ASH:
"Fuck, we gotta get outta here."

The ZOMBIES broke in. ASH began to shoot
them.

ASH:
"Go!"

SETH grabbed BUFFY and they headed out
the side door and down the hall. ASH and
JAMES headed to the ladder, toward the
roof. ASH began to climb. JAMES tried to
follow but the ZOMBIES grabbed him and
began biting his legs.

JAMES:
"Help!"

ASH:
"James!"

ASH leaned over and grabbed JAMES'S
hand.

ASH:
"Come on!"

JAMES:
"Don't let go! Don't let go!"

There were too many ZOMBIES. They pulled
JAMES down the ladder.

JAMES:
"No! Help me!"

The ZOMBIES pulled him down and consumed
him. Then a ZOMBIE began to climb the
ladder. ASH slammed the hatch shut. The
ZOMBIES began to rip JAMES apart. They
tore in to his stomach and began pulling
out his intestines. Another bit the side
of his face pulling his cheek off.

SETH and BUFFY heard JAMES'S screams as they headed toward the emergency exit. When they open the door they were greeted by a MAN with a shotgun. It as SAVINI!

SAVINI:
"Get down!"

SETH and BUFFY ducked.

SAVINI shot the ZOMBIE and it flew back.

<u>DINOSAUR VALLEY/NIGHTTIME</u>:

SAVINI:
"Get in!"

SETH and BUFFY jumped in to the truck and looked out the back window. They saw four men with guns shooting the ZOMBIES. Then one pulled out a container full of liquid. He lit it, and then threw it at the ZOMBIES. They soon became walking balls of flame.

SAVINI:
"Let's get out of here."

The four men got into vehicles. One got into the same pickup truck as SETH and BUFFY. Two others jumped onto a motorcycle with a side rider. The other got into an eighteen-wheeler with a huge box trailer full of supplies.

<u>LUCIO'S APIZZA ROOFTOP/NIGHTTIME:</u>

The ZOMBIES came up through the hatch.
ASH began shooting them.

ASH:
"Come on you fuckers!"

CLICK, CLICK, CLICK. He ran out of
bullets.

ASH:
"Fuck me."

He threw his gun and it hit a ZOMBIE
straight in the head. ASH then heard a
truck engine start up and ran to the
edge of the roof. He saw some people
beginning to take off.

<u>OUTSIDE LUCIO'S APIZZA/NIGHTTIME:</u>

The ZOMBIES that were on fire began to
reach the propane tanks.

<u>LUCIO'S APIZZA ROOFTOP/NIGHTTIME:</u>

ASH looked down and saw the semi-truck
driving by. He stepped back and knew he
had to time this just right. He then ran
passed the ZOMBIES pushing them aside.
He jumped off the roof just as the
propane tanks exploded. He landed on the
roof of the trailer and ended up rolling
when he landed. He rolled too far and
went off of the trailer. He grabbed the
back ladder and tried to hold on.

When the truck turned ASH lost his grip
and fell in the center green of the
valley.

DINOSAUR VALLEY/NIGHTTIME:

The truck kept driving and ASH got up,
there were ZOMBIES everywhere.

ASH:
"Fuck me sideways."

He pushed the ZOMBIES out of his way and
began to make his way to the police
precinct.

PICKUP TRUCK/NIGHTTIME:

SETH began to talk to SAVINI.

SETH:
"Thank you. We really appreciate this."

SAVINI:
"No problem. We didn't think there was
anyone still around."

SETH:
"What do you mean?"

SAVINI:
"Whatever is goin on, it's happening
everywhere on the island."

SETH:
"Are you serious?"

SAVINI:
"Like a heart attack."

SETH:
"We have to find my brother. He's still
out there."

SAVINI:
"Sorry no can do. This place is crawling
with those things. We need to get back
as soon as possible."

SETH was really upset at this response.

SAVINI:
"Look maybe he made and he'll find his
way to us. But we can't spare the time t
o look for him. We have to get these
supplies back to our group. I'm Savini
by the way."

Still upset SETH replied.

SETH:
"I'm Seth. This is Buffy."

SAVINI:
"Well Seth, I think you're gonna like
where you're gonna stay."

SETH:
"Where's that?"

SAVINI:
"The high school out in Cunningham.
There's a bunch of us there, and you
guys are more than welcome to stay."

SETH:
"Thanks. So you're the ones with the
flares the past few weeks?"

SAVINI:
"That's us. We noticed on the first
night that they were attracted to them.
So we used them to distract them while
we grabbed supplies. You're in good
hands now. You can rest easy."

SETH gave a sign of relief and sat back.
He then looked out the window seeing all
the zombies roaming around and became
worried about Ash.

DINOSAUR VALLEY POLICE PRECINCT/NIGHTTIME:

ASH came crashing through door, then
turned around and shut it. He fell back
and leaned up against the wall. Then he
shouted out.

ASH:
"Curtis!"

There was no response. He slowly got up
and began to look around. He heard some
munching noise coming from HOOPER'S
office. He entered and walked around the
desk and saw LAURIE. She was dead and
still being eaten by the little boy.

ASH:
"Shit."

The boy quickly jumped up and attacked
ASH.

They fell over the desk, ASH put his
hands around the little boy's head with
a firm grip. Then twisted it causing a
sicking snapping sound breaking the neck
in two. He then kicked the little boy
back. He sat there listening to the
ZOMBIES banging outside trying to get
in. He sat there quietly then just broke
down.

**CUNNINGHAM, JOHN LANDIS HIGH
SCHOOL/NIGHTTIME:**

SETH and BUFFY, they were walking with
SAVINI and came upon a room.

SAVINI:
"Well here's your room. Enjoy your
stay."

He gave a glance at BUFFY and walked off.
She was quiet and SETH looked at her.

SETH:
"You ok?"

There was no response.

SETH:
"Why don't you get some sleep."

SETH brought her to the bed and then she
laid down. SETH looked out the window
and stared out at the moon.

<u>**CHAPTER 9:**</u>

<u>**DINOSAUR VALLEY POLICE PRECINCT/MORNING:**</u>

ASH was sleeping and then woke up to a radio voice going off.

RADIO:
"Hello anyone out there? This is Savini, if there is anyone out there please head to John Landis High School in Cunningham. There are survivors."

ASH grabbed the radio and began to talk.

ASH:
"Hello? Hello, this is officer Redfield. I'm in the Dinosaur Valley police precinct and I need help. Those things are everywhere….."

He looked down and realized that the radio wasn't responding.

ASH:
"Fuck!"

He threw the microphone. He looked around then began to gather up all the weapons and ammo he could. Then he took a set of keys off of LAURIE'S body

<u>**OUTSIDE DINOSAUR VALLEY/MORNING:**</u>

As ASH walked out of the police precinct, the ZOMBIES that were in the area began to approach him. He pulled out his shotgun and began shooting them. BLAM! BLAM!

He made every shot a head shot, dropping
them like flies. He made his way towards
a police car. He jumped into a car and
began drive off. As he headed to the
school he looked out the car window. He
saw the ZOMBIES walking around looking
for food. He couldn't believe the amount
of destruction they caused.

JOHN LANDIS HIGH SCHOOL/AFTERNOON:

SETH was walking down a hallway looking
to see where everyone was. He heard some
noises coming from the main office. He
walked up and peeked in. There were
three men in the office. He saw SAVINI
and FATHER ROMERO talking.

FATHER ROMERO:
"Those new people will make fine
additions to our groups future."

SAVINI:
"One is the man from the Bar a while
back. The one with the non believer
brother."

FATHER ROMERO:
Ah yes, the lawman.

SAVINI:
"He wants to go back and look for him.
Apparently they got separated last
night."

FATHER ROMERO:
"We shall see if the lord has a plan for
them. Remember he works in mysterious
ways.

Maybe his brother can help us in our new
world."

FATHER ROMERO had a knife in his hands.

SAVINI:
"And if they refuse to join our cause?"

FATHER ROMERO:
"If they refuse, they shall be
sacrificed in the name of the lord
almighty, and until we can deal with his
wrath."

SETH couldn't believe what he heard and
he backed up, his shoes made a squeaking
noise. The FATHER ROMERO looked at
QUENTIN.

FATHER ROMERO:
"We're not alone."

He pointed to three other men and they
walked out of the room. SETH entered his
room with BUFFY.

SETH:
"Come on we gotta get going."

BUFFY just sat there quiet, SETH grabbed
her by her arm pulling her up.

SETH:
"Come on!"

They made it to the door. WHAM! SETH
fell back. QUENTIN was standing in the
door way with three other guys.

QUENTIN:
"Take him away."

The three other guys grabbed SETH.
QUENTIN then approached BUFFY. He
grabbed her and pushed her on the bed.

QUENTIN:
"I'll deal with her."

He jumped on top of her and began to
pull off her shirt. She didn't even try
to fight back. The other three guys took
SETH out of the room. QUENTIN began to
undo his pants. Suddenly his was pulled
off of her. He turned around and saw
that it was SAVINI and the FATHER
ROMERO.

FATHER ROMERO:
"What are you doing? She's our new
sister, you can't lay with her. Not
until you are one in matrimony."

QUENTIN:
"Well by our equal laws no man can deny
me the spoils of the new world."

SAVINI:
"He speaks the truth, Father Romero."

FATHER ROMERO pulled out his knife. He
looked at QUENTIN. SHUNK! QUENTIN
slumped forward then fell on the ground.
FATHER ROMERO then pulled the knife on
SAVINI.

FATHER ROMERO:
"Are you challenging me? Must I remind
you that I was left in charge by god.
And trust me when I say you don't want
to feel is wrath."

He pointed the knife at SAVINI'S bottom
jaw.

FATHER ROMERO:
"As long as my heart beats I am at the
lords call, so you keep your mouth shut
unless I speak to you."

He looked down at QUENTIN, then back to
SAVINI.

FATHER ROMERO:
"Put him with the others."

SAVINI:
"What about her?"

FATHER ROMERO:
"Leave her for now, she'll join us
tonight."

SAVINI:
"Yes, Father."

SAVINI began to drag QUENTIN'S body.
Then they walked out of the room and
shut the door.

OUTSIDE JOHN LANDIS HIGH SCHOOL/AFTERNOON:

ASH finally made it to the school.

There were no ZOMBIES around. He grabbed
his shotgun and proceeded to walk toward
the school.

INSIDE JOHN LANDIS HIGH SCHOOL/AFTERNOON:

He entered and didn't see anyone.

ASH:
"Anybody home?"

There was no answer. He continued to
walk down the hall. He saw a huge plaque
on a wall. He looked at all the names of
the teachers on it. There was a huge
picture of the principal. His name was
J.R. BOOKWALTER. ASH then walked down
the stairs to see if anyone was there.
When he got there he heard some voices
coming from a class room. He peeked in
the window and couldn't believe what he
saw. There was a young girl who looked
middle-eastern. She tied up and lying on
a table. FATHER ROMERO was standing
above her. She was screaming as he held
up a knife.

FATHER ROMERO:
"With your sacrifice our sins will be
cleansed!"

He took the knife and rammed it into her
chest. ASH was shocked. He kicked in the
door.

ASH:
"What the fuck is going on!"

He pointed the shotgun at the FATHER
ROMERO.

ASH:
"Answer me!"

WHACK! ASH fell down. Behind him was
SAVINI. In his hands were a set of brass
knuckles.

FATHER ROMERO
"Put him with the other one. We can't
let him interfere with our holy mission."

<u>**CHAPTER 10:**</u>

<u>**OUTSIDE CUNNINGHAM WOODS/LATE AFTERNOON:**</u>

ASH came around and woke up. He realized he was outside stripped off all his weapons. Also tied up to a tree but wasn't alone. He saw SETH tied up next up him.

ASH:
"Seth?"

SETH:
"Ash, you're alive?"

ASH:
"What the hell is going on?"

He started too look around to see where they were. He was trying to loosen the rope around him and SETH.

SETH:
"I don't have a fucking clue. I walked in on some sort of ritual talk and then found myself here."

ASH:
"Me too. What are they gonna do with us?"

SETH:
"The Old Man said something about cleansing our souls."

ASH:
"He won't have one when I'm done with him."

He looked around and didn't see BUFFY
anywhere.

ASH:
"Where's Buffy?"

SETH:
"I don't know? They brought her
somewhere. She's completely lost it."

Then FATHER ROMERO and SAVINI walked up
with three other men.

FATHER ROMERO:
"So if it isn't the non believer and the
lawman?"

ASH:
"Non believer? What the fuck are you
talking about?"

FATHER ROMERO:
"I have been chosen by the Holy One
himself to clean this new world and
bring a new order. If he wishes to kill
us with our own kind then so be it."

ASH:
"What? Where's Buffy?"

FATHER ROMERO:
"The Lord has chosen to erase the sins of
human with the dead."

ASH:
"Well who died and left you in charge?"

FATHER ROMERO:
"The Lord did, with a vision. He spoke
to me and told me that the end is near.
I told you officer that the end of days
was coming. But you chose to ignore it.
And that we need to prepare. And the
only way to do so is to sacrifice the
sinners. With each one it brings us
closer to salvation."

ASH:
(Sarcastically)
"It brings you closer to madness.
Where's Buffy!"

FATHER ROMERO:
"Buffy, Buffy. You sound like a broken
record player."

He paused for a moment.

FATHER ROMERO:
"We need fresh blood for the future.
But, I'll tell you what? I'll give you a
choice, you can either help us or join
this sinner in damnation?"

ASH:
"Is that multiple choice?"

SAVINI walked up and gave ASH a violent
uppercut. Then grabbed him by the throat
and began to choke him.

SAVINI:
"Answer him faggot!"

ASH:
"Ok, ok, alright, just one question
first?"

ASH spit out blood, then looked at
FATHER ROMERO and he nodded.

ASH:
"If I join you do I get my fair share of
little boys too, or do I have to get
them in stock. Or is there some sort of
fuck and release program?"

SAVINI punched ASH again, this time ASH
blacked out.

FATHER ROMERO:
"Leave them, they shall be dealt with.
Now let's get ready for the sermon. We
will be even more powerful with the
sacrifices of these two. The Day of
Reckoning is upon us Savini, we need to
cleanse the new world, for peace and
prosperity."

SAVINI:
"Any patrols?"

FATHER ROMERO:
"Put The Raimi's on duty."

SAVINI:
"Yes."

FATHER ROMERO:
"Six billion cries of agony will birth
the new balance. To bad they will not
live to see it."

They walked off. SETH tried to wake up
ASH.

SETH:
"Ash? Ash, hey wake up."

There was no response. Then he noticed
some ZOMBIES walking around.

SETH:
"Come on, wake up."

ASH began to come around.

SETH:
"Yeah come on, pull it together."

ASH:
"Whoa." (Shaking His Head) "Any calls
while I was out?"

SETH:
"We have some company."

ASH looked and saw a ZOMBIE.

ASH:
"Wow, that's a problem."

SETH:
"No shit. How do we get loose?"

ASH:
"Keep rubbing the rope against the tree."

They began to rub the rope back and
forth. The ZOMBIE got closer. When it
did it looked a lot like ROB ZOMBIE.

It got close to SETH.

SETH:
"Ash, how's it coming?"

ASH:
"Almost there."

The "ROB" ZOMBIE got even closer. The
zombie then stopped and went limp. SETH
looked at the confused for a moment. The
ZOMBIE was then ripped in half! Behind
it was another ZOMBIE, but this one was
different. It was larger and more
grotesque looking CREATURE with a claw
on one hand. It got closer to the both
of them, and let out a roar.

SETH:
"Ash. Ash!"

ASH got loose and grabbed a thick
branch. He smashed it against CREATURE.
The branch shattered in pieces. ASH
looked shocked and the CREATURE hit him,
sending him flying back.

SETH:
"Ash!!"

ASH slowly got up and saw the creature
within reach of SETH. ASH looked around
to see what he could find as a weapon.
He saw a rock and quickly grabbed it. He
threw it as hard as he could at the
CREATURES face, knocking it back. He
then ran and jumped on top of it.
ASH then grabbed the rock and began
bashing in the CREATURES face in.

Eventually he stopped because all he was
doing was smashing wet pieces of skull
into the ground. He then just sat there
out of breath. ASH then turned, walked
up and untied SETH.

SETH:
"Thanks, now come on we gotta get Buffy."

SETH began to walk off.

ASH:
"Why?"

SETH stopped in his tracks.

SETH:
"What do you mean why? Cause you made
her a promise. And I'm not leaving her
here with these lunatics."

ASH:
"The dock is right there, in a few
minutes we can be on Mikhail's boat and
leave this mess behind."

SETH:
"You're kidding right? Please tell me
you're fucking kidding?"

ASH:
"What? She's gone and we have our chance,
let's take it!"

SETH punched ASH right in the face. He
couldn't believe what his brother was
saying. He never thought that ASH would
act like this.

ASH:
"What the fuck is the matter with you!"

SETH:
"Me? What's the matter with you? Since
when is it in you to leave someone
behind? Look I'm sure you went through
hell while you were gone, but we went
through hell as well! Especially Me and
Diana! Why do you think she left?"

ASH:
"Why did you stick around? If I'm such
damaged goods, then why the hell are you
still around?"

SETH:
"Cuz you're my brother!"

ASH stood there for a moment, then he
looked at SETH. Just like the other
night with BUFFY, ASH realized how much
of an asshole he had been. He fell to
his knees

ASH:
"You're right. You're absolutely right.
I've been such an asshole."

SETH walked up to him. ASH looked up at
him.

ASH:
"Alright. Let's do it. Let's go get
her."

SETH:
"Really?"

SETH extended his hand to ASH.

ASH:
"Yes. You're right. But let's hurry and
get off this goddam island."

HE helped him up.

SETH:
"Fuckin A."

They began to walk off into the woods.

**OUTSIDE THE LOMBARDI HOUSE/LATE
AFTERNOON:**

Soon they made it to an old farm house.
The name on the mailbox read "LOMBARDI".

SETH:
"Hey it's old man Lombardi's. You think
he's home?"

ASH:
"Doubt it, but let's take a look around
anyway. I'm gonna check it out, you stay
here and shout if you see anything."

SETH:
"Be quick."

ASH entered the house and SETH waited
outside.

INSIDE THE LOMBARDI HOUSE/LATE AFTERNOON:

ASH was looking around.

ASH:
"Hello? Anyone there? It's officer Redfield."

He walked from room to room and found nothing. He then looked above the fire place. He saw a red machete on the wall. He walked up and grabbed it and it's holder. He put the holder on and held the machete.

<u>OUTSIDE THE LOMBARDI HOUSE/LATE AFTERNOON:</u>

SETH was standing when he heard a noise from a bush. He went to go investigate it. He walked up to the bush and out jumped a cat. It was Mr. WHISKERS. SETH gave a sigh of relief.

SETH:
"Fucking cat."

He turned around and headed back to the house, but as he did he was attacked by a ZOMBIE! It was OLD MAN LOMBARDI. He grabbed SETH and tackled him to the ground.

<u>INSIDE THE LOMBARDI HOUSE/LATE AFTERNOON:</u>

ASH heard the ruckus and headed out the door. As he made it out he was grabbed buy another ZOMBIE. It was an old female. She began chomping at ASH. He threw her back. He pulled out the machete and swung it. It took her head right off.

<u>**OUTSIDE THE LOMBARDI HOUSE/LATE**</u>
<u>**AFTERNOON:**</u>

SETH was still struggling with OLD MAN
LOMBARDI, SETH tried to overpower him
but OLD MAN LOMBARDI was overcome with
hunger. He took a huge chunk of flesh
out of SETH'S neck. SETH let out a
violent yell and looked at OLD MAN
LOMBARDI. CHOP! OLD MAN LOMBARDI'S head
went flying. SETH saw ASH standing with
the machete in his hand. ASH looked at
SETH who was choking on his blood.

ASH:
"Shit! Seth hold on okay, hold on."

SETH:
"Fuck! Fuck!"

ASH sat down placing the machete on the
ground. Then he put SETH'S head on his
lap.

ASH:
"Don't look at it, look at me. SETH!
Look at me!"

SETH:
(Choking) "It wasn't supposed to happen
like this, it wasn't supposed to be like
this."

ASH:
"It's my fault, ok? It's my fault."

SETH:
(Crying And Choking) "Ash, I don't wanna
be walking around like
that! Please……"

ASH sat there quietly.

SETH:
"I don't wanna die……."

SETH began grabbing ASH tight trying to
hold his hand.

ASH:
"You're not gonna die."

SETH:
"You're not gonna leave me, are you Ash?"

ASH:
"I'm right here buddy, I'm not going
anywhere."

SETH laid there on ASH'S lap. ASH was
trying to hold back his tears.

SETH:
"Please promise me you'll save BUFFY and
anyone else you find. Don't give up,
please promise me."

ASH:
"I promise. I promise I'll get her."

SETH reached over grabbing the machete
and handing it to ASH.

SETH:
"Kill me."

ASH:
"What?"

ASH was shocked at what his brother just
told him to do.

SETH:
"Kill me."

ASH:
"No, I can't"

SETH:
"Please, I don't wanna be one of them……"

ASH nodded and then got on his knees,
held the machete up high. A tear rolled
down the side of his face. He hesitated
for a moment. Then he rammed the machete
into SETH'S chest. Blood squirted like a
hose into the air. ASH then pulled the
machete out. He slowly got up and stood
there for a moment. Then threw the
machete.

ASH:
"Fuck! Fuck! Fuck!"

He began kicking OLD MAN LOMBARDI'S dead
body. Then he fell down to his knees and
began to break down. After a few seconds
he stood up and shook it off. He grabbed
the machete and ran off into the woods
toward the school. Over by SETH'S body,
his hand began to twitch, then his eyes
opened wide.

CHAPTER 11:

OUTSIDE JOHN LANDIS HIGH SCHOOL/LATE AFTERNOON:

ASH finally got the school, but he noticed three men standing there on patrol. They were SAM, TED, and IVAN. The RAIMI'S They were all talking and SAM was picking his nails. ASH knew he had to play it quiet. He slowly came up from behind as TED and IVAN began to walk away. ASH grabbed SAM by the neck and snapped it. TED and IVAN both turned around. ASH then threw his machete it at TED, it hit him right in the chest. IVAN went to attack ASH but ASH grabbed him. ASH flipped IVAN over. Then stomped on his neck crushing it like a soda can. ASH looked at them and shook his head. He pulled the machete out of TED'S chest.

ASH:
"Fucking stooges."

INSIDE JOHN LANDIS HIGH SCHOOL/EARLY AFTERNOON:

ASH headed back to the same class room as before. But this time there wasn't anyone there. ASH looked around, he turned a corner. He saw SAVINI walking around the hall, ASH then hid. SAVINI was holding a shotgun and walking. Then he stopped at the end of the hall. He looked down both sides and saw nothing. He then turned around. WHAM! He was hit in the face.

He staggered back and when he came too
he saw ASH. SAVINI smiled and went on
the attack.

SAVINI:
"I've been waiting for this moment!"

He began to unleash his fists on ASH.
ASH was blocking but missed one block.
He fell back into the hallway. The
shotgun went in one direction. ASH'S
machete in another. ASH went to grab the
machete. But SAVINI grabbed him by the
leg and threw him into the lockers. He
picked ASH up. ASH head butted SAVINI.
SAVINI stumbled back with ASH beginning
pummeling him. ASH had the upper hand
until SAVINI low blowed him. ASH fell
down by the machete. As SAVINI grabbed
ASH, ASH grabbed the machete and rammed
it into SAVINI'S stomach. SAVINI went
limp. ASH pulled the machete up from
SAVINI'S stomach to his throat. He
pulled it out and swung cutting SAVINI'S
throat.

JOHN LANDIS HIGH SCHOOL AUDITORIUM/LATE AFTERNOON:

FATHER ROMERO was there with about
twenty to thirty people. BUFFY stood
next to him.

There were two other men in cloaks
standing behind her.

FATHER ROMERO:
"Now I welcome our new sister, Buffy to
our family."

Someone got up and headed towards the
doors. He raised his hands and everyone
stood up.

FATHER ROMERO:
"We are the future of this planet. I am
your god and you are all my children."

They all began to cheer and scream.
SMASH! The door was then kicked in. The
person in front of the door flew back.
It was ASH and he had SAVINI'S shotgun.
He pointed it right at FATHER ROMERO.

ASH:
"Freeze!"

FATHER ROMERO looked up very surprised.

FATHER ROMERO:
"Why do you continue to fight me? Do you
really believe I can be stopped?"

ASH:
"Either way I'm not gonna stop until I'm
dead."

FATHER ROMERO:
"Then I'll have to kill you quickly.
Seize him!"

A few people got up and approached ASH.

ASH:
"Listen, I'm just here for the woman.
But I am willing to take anyone else
with me. I'm leaving this island for the
main land. Anyone want to come is more
than welcome."

FATHER ROMERO:
"And where would you go? The dead are
everywhere."

ASH:
"I don't know, but I've got to try."

FATHER ROMERO:
"What if we refuse? Will you kill us?"

ASH:
"I just want to take her. I don't want
to kill anyone, but I will if I have
too."

FATHER ROMERO:
"He won't kill us"

ASH:
"Look padre I've killed more than a
dozen people within the last few days
and if you think that cause you're a man
of god I won't kill you, then you're
sadly mistaken."

One PERSON approached ASH

MAN:
"How dare you step foot in this holy
place!"

The MAN puled out a tiny bade from his
robe. BLAM! ASH shot him, straight into
the chest sending him flying back. Then
he pointed the gun at FATHER ROMERO.

ASH:
"I got no problem killing you. "

FATHER ROMERO:
"That was a man of God!"

ASH:
"Not my God! What gives you the right to
say who's a sinner? You're killing
innocent people. Isn't that a sin. Thou
shall not kill?"

FATHER ROMERO:
"The human race requires judgment."

ASH:
"And you're going to judge us? Do you
get all your ideas from comic book
villains?"

FATHER ROMERO:
"Has it ever occurred to you that this
planet is over populated? Only a hand
full of humans truly matter. Everyone
else is weak. Now we must separate the
weak from the strong."

ASH:
"Who are the weak? Who are the strong?"

FATHER ROMERO:
"The strong are those who are those who
don't give in to temptation. The weak
are the men who share their beds with
other men, the unfaithful whores who
cheat on their husbands, the niggers
who come to our land and take that
doesn't belong to them. We are the few
who must now face these dark times with
each other and continue the road to
prosperity."

ASH:
"Listen to yourself?"

FATHER ROMERO:
"Those who refuse to do gods work must
die as an example!"

ASH just stood there in shock. How can a
man of GOD act like this? Has he truly
gone mad?

FATHER ROMERO:
(He Pointed To His People) "Now get
him!"

Everyone got up and approached him. He
held the shotgun up and pointed it at
them.

ASH:
"This is madness."

They kept coming until they surrounded
him completely.

ASH:
"Get Back!"

FATHER ROMERO:
"The only madness is the blasphemy you
are inflicting upon these holy followers
of the Lord."

One guy got close to ASH. ASH pointed
the gun right at the guy's nose.

ASH:
"Go ahead, try it!"

The PERSON stepped back. BLAM! ASH fired
his gun into the air and made his way to
BUFFY.

ASH:
"Buffy."

There was no response from her, she was
still in a trance.

ASH:
"Damn it! What the hell did you do to
her?"

FATHER ROMERO:
"She saw the light and you will too.
You're simply postponing the
inevitable."

ASH was grabbed from behind by some of
the followers. They grabbed the shotgun
out of his hands, then tackled him to
the ground. He tried to fight back but
there were too many of them.

ASH looked up at BUFFY.

ASH:
"Buffy, it's me Ash, snap out of it!"

FATHER ROMERO:
"Everyday mankind grows closer and
closer to its self destruction."

ASH somehow managed to fight the
followers off. He rolled over and
grabbed the shotgun. FATHER ROMERO
pulled out a small handgun.

FATHER ROMERO:
"I'm not destroying the world, I'm
merely saving it. Then, behold, the veil
of the temple was torn in two from top
to bottom; and the earth quaked, and the
rocks were split, and the graves were
opened; and many bodies of the dead who
had fallen were raised; and coming out
of the graves after his resurrection,
they went into the cities and appeared
to many."

ASH turned around and pointed the
shotgun at FATHER ROMERO.

ASH:
"I've had enough of your bullshit!"

Soon both gun's were pointed at each
other. FATHER ROMERO'S was at ASH'S
head. ASH'S shotgun was pointed at
FATHER ROMERO'S chest.

FATHER ROMERO:
"You really think you can kill me?"

ASH:
"You don't have the right to play god!"

FATHER ROMERO:
"The right to play god?" (Pausing) "That
right is now mine."

ASH looked up at FATHER ROMERO. There
was a shadow behind him in the stained
glass window.

FATHER ROMERO:
"We're all going to ascend together, in
to the Lord's loving arms."

ASH:
"Really? More like his arms."

FATHER ROMERO:
"Huh?"

SMASH! Hands came through the window.
They grabbed FATHER ROMERO and pulled
him outside. The ZOMBIE that attacked
him was SETH. He bit FATHER ROMERO in
the neck pulling out a huge chunk of
flesh. Then the other ZOMBIES began to
attack him too. They dug their fingers
into his stomach tearing into his flesh.
One grabbed his hand and began to bite
off his fingers. As he was screaming
another ZOMBIE dug its finger nail into
his eyes. They began to pull the skin
off, his eyes rolled out of his head A
ZOMBIE picked the eyes up and bit it.
Then the rest of the ZOMBIES began to
enter. The other people sat there and
let the ZOMBIES eat them. ASH couldn't
believe his eyes. He ran up to BUFFY and
untied her.

ASH:
"Buffy, come on."

ZOMBIES approached the two of the them.
BLAM! ASH sent them flying back. ASH
grabbed her and they ran off out the
side door.

JOHN LANDIS HIGH SCHOOL HALLWAY/LATE AFTERNOON:

Down the hallway the ZOMBIES we're coming from everywhere. ASH looked in a class and saw a window.

ASH:
"This way."

He and BUFFY entered the classroom.

JOHN LANDIS HIGH SCHOOL CLASS ROOM/LATE AFTERNOON:

ASH put the teacher's desk in front of the door. The ZOMBIES began to pound and bang on the door.

ASH:
"Come on,We gotta get the fuck out of here."

BUFFY finally came to her senses.

BUFFY:
(Weary) "Ash?"

ASH:
(Relieved) "Yes, it's me."

BUFFY:
"Where am I?"

ASH:
"Long story. Are you ok?"

BUFFY:
"I'm not sure."

ASH:
"The marina isn't far from here. And we
need to get going, now."

BUFFY:
"How?"

ASH smashed the window with the shotgun
then he and BUFFY jumped out. Then the
ZOMBIES came crashing through the door.

CHAPTER 12:

CUNNINGHAM WOODS/LATE AFTERNOON:

ASH and BUFFY entered the woods. They kept running until they finally reached the marina.

DINOSAUR VALLEY MARINA/LATE AFTERNOON:

ASH saw MIKHAIL'S boat.

ASH:
"There, the Argento."

They both made their way to the boat.

INSIDE THE ARGENTO/LATE AFTERNOON

They got inside it.

ASH:
"Let's get this thing going."

ASH went to start up. CLICK, CLICK, CLICK. The boat but it wouldn't start.

ASH:
"Now what?"

BUFFY entered the cabin. ASH held his head down.

BUFFY:
"What's wrong?"

ASH:
"I don't know? It won't work."

He looked at the fuel and it was dry.

ASH:
"Come on!"

He kicked the counter. Then he sat in
the chair.

ASH:
"I failed everyone. I promised… I
promised to get you all too fucking
safety and instead I got you all
killed."

BUFFY:
"It's not your fault."

ASH:
"It is my fault! It's my fault… maybe
Eric was right. We should've just stayed
put, then everyone would still be
alive."

He just sat there. SMACK! BUFFY slapped
ASH across the face.

BUFFY:
"Fuck you! If anyone should be upset
right now it should be me. I lost my
daughter, my husband, and was almost
raped. You need to man the fuck up and
get this boat working to get us the fuck
out of here. Now!"

ASH got up, looked at BUFFY and smiled.

OUTSIDE THE ARGENTO/LATE AFTERNOON

He ran off the boat and looked at the
fuel tanks. He grabbed the pump, he
began to fill it up.

ASH:
"Try it now."

INSIDE THE ARGENTO/LATE AFTERNOON

BUFFY started the boat and it worked.

BUFFY:
"Yes! It worked!"

OUTSIDE THE ARGENTO/LATE AFTERNOON

ASH dropped the pump and headed to the
boat. But his leg was grabbed from under
the dock. He fell and looked behind him.
There was a ZOMBIE. It was CHAZ, he
jumped at ASH.

INSIDE THE ARGENTO/LATE AFTERNOON

BUFFY went to see what happened to ASH.
She saw him fighting with CHAZ. ASH was
trying to reach his gun. BUFFY went to
help but was stopped by another ZOMBIE.
This one was A.J. She screamed and ran
inside the cabin locking the doors
behind her.

OUTSIDE THE ARGENTO/LATE AFTERNOON:

ASH managed to push CHAZ back and grab
his shotgun. He shot CHAZ in the side of
the face blowing it completely off.

INSIDE THE ARGENTO/LATE AFTERNOON

A.J. smashed the door window of the
cabin and pushed the door opened. Before
he could grab BUFFY he was grabbed and
thrown out the door.

OUTSIDE THE ARGENTO/LATE AFTERNOON

A.J. got back up. ASH ran and tackled
him. They both went over the rail. ASH
got up first. ASH looked and saw an ice
hook then grabbed it. He then hit A.J.
in the bottom of the jaw and yanked it
right off. He then kicked A.J. off the
deck into the water. ASH looked off the
deck and up in the boat at BUFFY. She
then looked and saw about thirty ZOMBIES
heading their way.

BUFFY:
"Time to go."

ASH grabbed his shotgun and then ran to
the gas pump.

BUFFY:
"What are you doing?"

ASH didn't answer. He just poured the
gas all over the tanks and then backed
up. He waited for the ZOMBIES to get
close enough. When they were he pointed
the shotgun at the tanks and fired.
BLAM! BOOM! The tanks exploded. The
ZOMBIES went everywhere. ASH flew back
into the water. BUFFY ran off the boat
and to the end of the deck.

BUFFY:
"Ash! Ash!"

She looked into the water. After a few
seconds ASH came popping out.

ASH:
(Coughing) "Why the hell did you let me
do that?"

She smiled. Then she helped him out of
the water.

BUFFY:
"You're a complete jack ass. You know
that, right?"

ASH:
"It seemed like a good idea at the
time."

They both got up and headed to the boat.
BLAM! There was a gun shot. ASH and
BUFFY couldn't believe who they saw. It
was EIRC but he wasn't his usual self.
He was a ZOMBIE! In his hand was a gun.
He as shambling and fired it again and
missed them. He couldn't keep his aim
steady do to the fact he was barely
function able.

ASH:
"Move!"

He pushed BUFFY out of the way and she
ran on the other side of the boat. BLAM!
ASH ducked and tried to hide. BLAM! He
fried again.

ASH noticed his Shotgun. He crawled
towards the shotgun. BLAM! ERIC fired
one more time. ASH then grabbed the
shotgun and pointed it at ERIC. ERIC had
his gun pointed a ASH. CLICK! Both guns
were empty. Nothing came out.

ASH:
"Of course."

ASH looked at the gun and gave a smirk.
ERIC jumped on ASH trying to bite him.
ASH used the shotgun to keep ERIC up.
BUFFY ran off. ERIC was chomping away
trying to get a piece of ASH. Blood was
pouring out of his mouth falling all
over ASH'S face. ASH thought to himself
that this was defiantly the end. He
closed him eyes and waited for it. TWIP!
ERIC'S body went limp. ASH opened his
eyes. He saw ERIC lifeless, there was an
arrow threw ERIC'S head. The arrow was
two inches from ASH'S face. ASH then
kicked ERIC back. BUFFY came running out
of the boat. ASH then looked at BUFFY
who didn't have any weapons. Then he
looked over at the other end of the dock
and saw MIKHAIL!His leg was wrapped and
he had a bow in his hand.

ASH:
"Mikhail!"

ASH got up and ran to him.

ASH:
"We thought you were dead."

MIKHAIL:
"I almost was."

ASH:
"What happened?"

MIKHAIL:
"After Eric shot me, those things broke
into the store and I hide behind a
couple of shelves and after a few hours
I heard a huge explosion and trucks
driving away. I tried to make my way to
the door but they were already gone and
I saw you running off. I didn't know
what was going on so I headed to the
marina and waited in the office for you
guys to show up. And when you did I was
on my way out when there was another
explosion."

ASH:
"Sorry about that."

BUFFY:
"Can we go now?"

ASH nodded. He helped MIKHAIL on to the
boat and into the cabin.

INSIDE THE ARGENTO/LATE AFTERNOON:

He started the boat and they began to
sail off.

MIKHAIL:
"Let's get the fuck outta here."

They sailed off, about an hour later they
were in the mainland.

MAINLAND/DUSK:

They pulled the boat ashore and got out.

CITY/DUSK:

They began to walk into the city looking around. It was quiet and there was no one around.

BUFFY:
"Where is every one?"

They walked and a news paper flew in the wind. One got stuck on ASH'S leg. He bent down, picking it up. He looked at it and his eyes opened wide. The front o f the paper read in big bold letters. THE DEAD WALK!

MIKHAIL:
"What? What is it?"

ASH dropped the paper and looked at them. They looked around and saw that there were cars littered, bodies in the street, windows smashed and buildings on fire. There was the sounds of loud moaning in the distance and silhouettes of the undead past the flames completely surrounding them.

ASH:
"It's everywhere."

                    THE END

www.ingramcontent.com/pod-product-compliance
Lightning Source LLC
Chambersburg PA
CBHW062144150726
47991CB00006B/2170